THE SHIELD OF ACHILLES

by James Forman

THE SKIES OF CRETE

RING THE JUDAS BELL

THE SHIELD OF ACHILLES

THE SHIELD OF ACHILLES

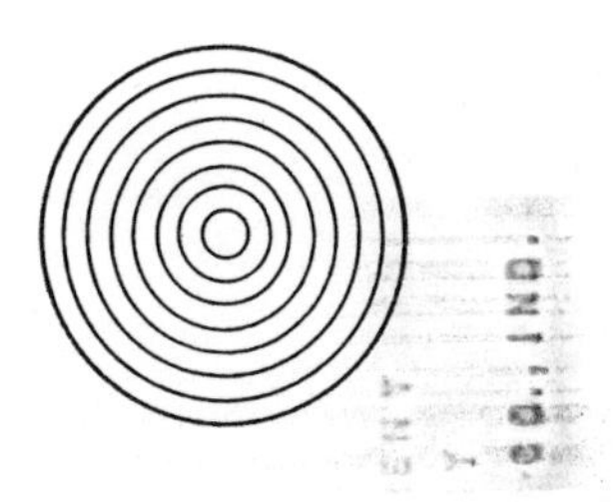

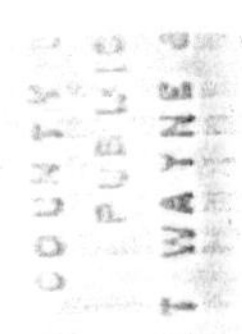

JAMES FORMAN

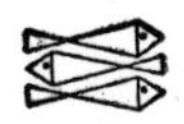

BELL BOOKS
Farrar, Straus and Giroux
New York

Library of Congress catalog card number 66–14036
First printing, 1966
Published simultaneously in Canada
by Ambassador Books, Ltd., Toronto
Printed in the United States of America
Bell Books is a division of Farrar, Straus & Giroux, Inc.

For Marcia,
who loves Cyprus
more than the natives do

THE SHIELD OF ACHILLES

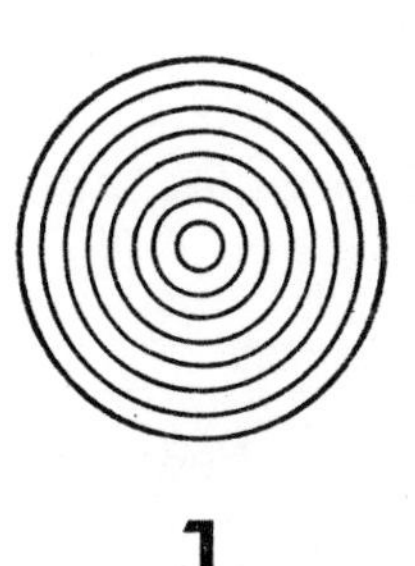

1

The sky was cloudless and remote. To the east lay distant mountains. Except where cedar forests drank up the light, they might have been part of the sky. The western horizon was filled with the Mediterranean Sea. Its waves seemed to be on fire.

Between the mountains and the sea, the land was rolling and dry. Occasional dusty carob trees dropped inky shadows, more substantial in the glare than the trees themselves. Stretching inland was a road. Under the blazing sun it looked rutted and uninviting. Nothing moved along the road, but where a whitewashed house and a small chapel cast a single heavy shadow, two figures were painting.

The more imposing was an angular, elderly monk. He would have given an impression of extreme height except for his posture—stooped shoulders and a long neck which seemed to have been broken and improperly reset. His companion was a girl. Not more than seventeen, she too was tall, with a mass of heavy black hair, a pale face and resolute mouth. Even when she was not painting, her dark eyes bore an expression of concentration.

The pair seldom spoke. They worked at their painting, but Eleni sang softly.

"Love hath an island
And I would be there.
Cyprus, Love's island,
And I would be there."

Father Grikos leaned back from his canvas, a complex scene of cities and battles carefully ruled out in the Byzantine tradition. He gave a disapproving sigh. Eleni knew it was meant for her, but she went on singing.

"At Paphos she dwelleth
And I would be there."

"Cyprus is God's island now, my dear," he reproached her.

Eleni looked at him, studied him. He was the patriarch of New Paphos, a great man descended from Joseph of Arimathea. He was not a gentle priest of the icons, but a fighting priest of patriotism and gunpowder. She could imagine him stoking the guns of Famagusta when the Turkish janissaries breached the walls. He was a fighter all right, and more. There was something about that flinty face with its vulture's beak of a nose that she could not fathom, as if it were unreconciled with another, inner face. Yes, as though God and the devil wrestled inside the man.

"It's a quiet afternoon," said Father Grikos.

"Yes. The heat."

As if in contradiction came a dull and distant thud. A spasm moved the air and a little lizard sunning itself on a stone wall darted for its hole like a flicker of green lightning.

Eleni, whose only apparent reaction was a tremor of her brush, felt a stirring of apprehension.

"Perhaps they're dynamiting for fish again," she said, and knew better.

A second explosion followed, more muffled than the first.

"Perhaps," said the priest. His every word received its full measure, like the tuning of an organ. Silence fell again, until there came the distant wailing of a siren; high, then soft, then high again, a kind of lamentation.

Sighting over his brush, Father Grikos said, "Good. Very good."

Eleni gave him a searching glance, and he seemed to anticipate her. "My dear, I mean your work. Honestly, it's quite good!" Thoughtfully he stroked his beard, then held her little painting at arm's length. His thick glasses made his eyes look small as he studied it, enormous when he looked at her. "What's this in the picture?" he asked.

"The Acropolis." It wasn't his criticism that concerned her now, but the sounds from the town of Ktima. "Do you know what's going on?" she asked him.

"Blue?" he said. "Why not paint it white, the way it is?"

All right. So he would not speak of the explosion, the siren. "Blue is the way I imagine it," she told him, and she imagined it passionately. Painting was to Eleni the only true way of possessing the world.

Father Grikos said, "Honestly, I don't want to bring evil

upon you with too much praise," and he pursed his lips as if to whistle. They resembled the suckers of a squid and were very moist. They did not belong with the rest of his face.

"Once you've seen it, you will paint it very differently," he assured her. She would be seeing it soon. In two weeks her scholarship began. "No, you don't paint things the way they are at all." His voice bore a note of indictment. Then he laughed. "But your blue Acropolis gives me pleasure. My opinion is that you will be a fine painter."

Eleni looked away, embarrassed with pride. She thought, "What a thoroughly great man he is."

"But you'll never be a religious painter," he said. She had no such intention. "There are certain rules. Look here . . . see what I've been doing. These black lines."

They both looked at Father Grikos's huge canvas, and Eleni, realizing enthusiasm was expected, voiced the appropriate compliment. It was entirely genuine. There was no doubt in her mind that Father Grikos was in the process of completing a masterpiece for the monastery at Chrysorroyiatissa. The painting itself was round, on a square canvas, and he called it "The Shield of Achilles." There were the heavens, the oceans, two cities, warring armies, the entire world as Hephaestus had inscribed it on the famous shield.

The monk sucked conscientiously on the end of his brush. As his long, blue-veined hands moved over the canvas, he described the shield to Eleni as he had done many times before. "This is our city, full of mourning. It's set off by these black lines. Then the Turks. I have to sketch them in first, and next the English. The battle will be here, and the victory here. Fighting may be a bad habit, but it's a grand one. There is no pleasure equal to triumphing over one's enemies." His words came like the beat of a pneumatic drill.

"What a strange man," thought Eleni. She both loved and feared him. She had never questioned the story that he slept in his own coffin to remind himself of his last rest.

"You know," he went on, "there's a kind of permission needed for war. It depends on the attitude of the people. I think we will have that permission soon. I can see the armies in the sky, their lances aimed in every ray of light. That's why I paint as I do. Someone has to keep the fire burning on the altar. I shan't let it go out."

Eleni knew this was a pledge Father Grikos would keep at the cost of his life and soul. But his was not the only life and soul involved in bringing Cyprus back to Greece. There were many more. They were there in his painting, and it worried her that his warriors did not bear shields and spears, but guns. Nor did they wear armor, but the tan of British uniforms, the motley of Greek and Turkish peasant clothes. And unlike the warriors of ancient Troy, there were no gods to save the heroes when they fell.

Behind the low hills a plane cracked and recracked the sound barrier. New Paphos was about forty miles from the British air base at Akrotiri, four minutes' flying time for the jet fighters. They came over with regularity. Eleni looked up into the glare but could not see the plane. She had not yet learned the trick of looking ahead of the sound.

"Holy Jesus and Mary, forgive us our sins, protect us from the evil eye," said Father Grikos, crossing himself and shaking his fist at the sky in one continuous gesture. To Eleni, he looked like a portrait of Moses about to smash the tablets. "I hate the airplane," he said. "It makes war hideous."

Eleni could not hate the planes so vehemently, for it was by plane that she would go to Athens, an English plane at that, and thanks to an English scholarship. Athens had been the dream of her life. Actually to go "over there," as so few Cypriotes had done, seemed almost too great a gift for her to bear alone. There was a story that the descendants of Zeus, on their way to eternity, halted over the Acropolis for one last look at the earth and realized that it was indeed a place of beauty and joy. The Acropolis of Athens was the heart of the world.

The afternoon might have passed in painting and conversation like so many other afternoons, but this day there was to be a difference. It began as a faint stirring of dust far down the road from Ktima. Had it not been for the explosions, Eleni would have paid no heed. Gradually a figure in the dust became perceptible: baggy blue trousers, white cotton shirt, pumping feet that left a waist-high cloud of dust. Though the figure was far off, Eleni recognized him by the way he sprang on the balls of his feet, light as a feather. It was Phaethon, a boy she had known since childhood. From a rough menace who threw stones at birds, he had turned into a beautiful young man. Beautiful was the word, for he was more than handsome, with hair so black it was startling, eyes clear and just as black. He was on the crest of youth, as her mother would say, a boy with spirit, who yearned for the union of Cyprus with Greece. Her mother said that he was a little drunk with patriotism, but Eleni thrilled to the quick footsteps clipping down the road, raising the dust. She expected a magnificent flash of white teeth, but Phaethon was nearer now, and unsmiling. His face was so pale that it exaggerated the darkness of his eyes; large, round eyes, the eyes of an animal.

"What's wrong?" she cried. He didn't seem to hear. Only then did she realize that he was terrified.

He arrived gasping, shivering.

Struggling for breath, he managed to say, "They're after me . . . dogs . . ."

"No!"

"They're after Stephan, too. I think they have him . . . God! I'm afraid of dogs." He was leaning on the stone fence with both hands. "If only I could get to the forest. . . . It's the dogs I'm afraid of."

"I'll do anything to help you, Phaethon, anything! You know that."

"Can you hide me here?" he asked her.

Father Grikos interrupted. "Absolutely not!"

"A gun, then, Eleni! Has your father a gun?"

"At the store. . . . That's a long way."

"Oh God, God!" The muscles of his face were tense with fear. His heavy black brows, always a little too high, as if in perpetual protest against life, seemed to meet across his forehead.

"Wait," she told him, and ran to the house. Inside, she snatched up an Italian stiletto her father had brought home from the war. When she returned, Phaethon was still leaning against the stone wall, eyes closed, lips moving, seemingly in prayer. He stood erect when he heard her.

"I'm cold," he said. She offered the knife, and he took it in trembling hands. "Look at me. I'm frightened to death." He seemed surprised at his admission. "Look at my hands."

"Where will you go?"

The answer was a while in coming, then only in a small secret voice.

"I know a place." He held her hand for an instant. "You shouldn't have anything to do with me. You ought to tell me to keep away from you. Eleni . . ."

"I want to help you, Phaethon. Tell me what I can do."

"Eleni," he whispered, "you know where I'll be. I'll need things tonight. Will you bring food? And a gun if you can? But come alone. Don't forget."

To all this, Father Grikos had listened attentively, head cocked to the side like a curious bird. Then, as though in possession of some private knowledge, he said, "You've done well, my boy, as any right-minded man with an atom of patriotism ought to do. Now go before they find you here, and be on your guard. Sleep with one eye open, as they say."

The boy gave Eleni's hand a final squeeze.

"Remember," he said, and turned away. He went down the road on light feet as silently as if he had been in the depths of the woods. His figure became small, merged with the dust, and was gone.

Father Grikos said, "God bless you, my son, in your labors of this day." He made the sign of the cross three times in the air.

For a while the dust hung over the road like a ghost, then blew away. Father Grikos sighed gustily. "You look troubled," he said.

She did not answer.

"There comes a time, Eleni, when men must do what they must."

Eleni knew this and she was proud of Phaethon, for she believed as he did that Cyprus should reunite with Greece. To share, however insignificantly, in his rebellion, gave her a kind of happiness. But what did they share, exactly? What had he done?

"Jesus preached love," said Father Grikos. "But first, fire and the axe. I'm very proud of that young man."

"What did he do?" she demanded.

"Whatever he did, I'm certain it was for Greece."

And whatever it was had turned him into a hunted animal. No, there was more of the child about him. In his moment of panic, he had looked absurdly young. He had been a child chased by the dark, and she wanted to mother him. Tonight she would take him food.

"Come along," said the monk. "Let's compose ourselves as though nothing has happened. The English will be here presently with their dogs, and we have been painting quietly all afternoon." He sat down, his penetrating eyes seeming to fix a demon a little to Eleni's left, and began to paint. She marveled at his composure. She knew he was right, but when she picked up the brush it wasn't steady between her fingers and it was hard to think of Athens.

Half an hour passed before the British came. They did not come with dogs, but drove up in a Land-Rover, leaving a column of dust as high as the treetops. Eleni asked God to make the lorry pass by, but it stopped. Then she asked God to make her calm, as though nothing had happened, when in fact her world had changed.

The car was full of big soldiers in khaki, well-fed men wearing the red berets of paratroopers. The one beside the driver got out. A tall man, slightly hunched and worried-looking, walked toward them. His hair was sandy red; angry hair, thought Eleni. She began to paint furiously.

The soldier stopped beside the whitewashed stone wall. He planted one hand firmly on the stone and seemed to be comparing the length of his fingers.

"*Kalimera,* Father Grikos," he said finally, in rough but intelligible Greek.

The monk looked up. "Lieutenant Hamley. I'm sorry. I didn't hear you arrive. When I paint, you know, I notice nothing."

"Of course," said the soldier. "With your permission, I'll visit your chapel."

"But of course, Lieutenant."

Nothing of what was going on beneath the surface showed in the manner of the two tall men, but Eleni felt a churning in her stomach.

The lieutenant directed four of his men to the chapel that stood across the road. Once a shrine to Aphrodite and now a chapel in memory of Saint Paul, who had been flogged nearby, it was small, a poor hiding place. The soldiers returned almost immediately. The lieutenant pointed out the house where Eleni and her father lived. It was the only other possible place of concealment nearby and it had to be searched.

Father Grikos leaned on an umbrella he held between his knees. "Of course, Lieutenant, but it's not my house." He turned to Eleni. The sun flashed from his glasses and behind them his eyes seemed hollow with mockery. "Eleni, I presume you'll show the gentlemen your house. They may enjoy your paintings." He made a little steadying gesture with the flat of his hand, a benediction.

Eleni walked with the lieutenant beside her, the men behind. She showed them first the main room, where two caged canaries sang in the rafters. It was a bare place; a few chairs, a large chest, a picture of her uncle who had been an evzone and a great hero, her parents' room, her own room, empty as a nun's cell except for the murals on the walls. The lieutenant called his soldiers to see the paintings. He said they were good, and Eleni would have felt pleasure were it not for the seriousness of the occasion.

Throughout the search she kept choosing certain things, not touching them but mentally setting them aside for Phaethon. She felt a fearful excitement as she plotted in the presence of the enemy.

The soldiers trudged back to the Land-Rover. "These are trying times, Lieutenant," said Father Grikos. "You know how it is, like Exodus. Caught one chapter away from Paradise!" Father Grikos laughed a loud ha-ha. The sound was jarring and the soldiers looked at him.

One of them said, "Yes, and you speak with the voice of the original serpent." The priest's mouth stayed open. At the corners of his mouth, his beard was darkly stained.

Eleni watched the hated, loved foreigners pull away and disappear into their own dust. A mixture of emotions rose inside her. But Father Grikos spat into the dust. He had only hate for the English.

Turning toward her, he held his beard in one hand as though about to tear it off. "I wish to heaven a priest's word had the power to kill," he said. "It's time to free our hearts of these British. Oh, yes, I'll be a serpent in their Eden for them." Then he seemed to collect himself. He cleared his throat and struck his umbrella against his thigh meditatively. "Well," he said; no more than that.

Eleni had no thought of painting. She wanted to get away, but Father Grikos was not ready for her to go. He had more to say. "That boy of yours is high-strung, but they don't make them any better."

"You mean Phaethon?"

"Of course, your fiancé."

"But he isn't exactly . . ."

Father Grikos leaned forward, smiling now, and patted her hand gently, understandingly. "But of course, my dear, of course. Still, he is handsome. 'God give me two more eyes,' that is what the girls say. And his father—what wealth! A branch on Ismail Pasha Street in Cairo, another in Alexandria—you don't know how lucky you are, my dear." He nodded continuously, as if with each nod to drive his point a little deeper. But all such thoughts were far from Eleni's mind. She wanted to know what was happening, she wanted sympathy, and she knew she would get neither from Father Grikos.

"I'm going to the pharmacy to see my father," she lied. Actually it was Raphael she wanted to see, as she always did when she was deeply troubled. From his skeptical grunts, she doubted that Father Grikos believed a word she was saying.

"The worst thing about Paphos, my dear, is that there simply isn't any refuge from gossip." The lines from Father

Grikos's nose to the corners of his mouth were as strong and deep as in ancient sculpture. "I feel sorry for that fisherman. I honestly do. It's a sad thing when a young man makes a hash of his life. But it's not up to you to get involved, my dear."

Raphael had not exactly made a hash of his life. Rather, he had made nothing of it whatsoever. What was more, he didn't seem to care. At times this infuriated Eleni as much as it did the priest, but unlike Father Grikos, she was deeply attached to the fisherman. He gave her a sense of gentle peace as no one else could do, and to protect their relationship from the priest, she lied again. "I wasn't going to see him, if that's what you mean."

"I'm glad. I knew you weren't. God grant that his soul may be saved." Not once had Raphael's name been pronounced. He was the young man, the outcast, whom Father Grikos had first hounded out of school and then on a day of terrible scandal had excommunicated from the Church of Cyprus. Eleni could not forget the priest in his white robes, the beadle with the holy water, and the terrible words, "Out from here! Out from here! Excommunicated!" Such was the penalty for all Greek Cypriotes who refused to vote for union with Greece. All save Raphael had done so, and when those words of anathema rang on the air it was as though the terrible ministers of God were actually advancing to hound him into hell. At the time it had seemed like the end for Raphael: he would surely have to disappear in shame. But his solitary life went on much as before, and Eleni could not shake off her affection for him.

"You know my high regard for you. Please don't do anything to spoil it," said the priest.

Eleni had the impulse to clap a hand over his mouth, but she had to sit there smiling and smiling and smiling. A change of posture might help; she stood up. "I really ought to go."

"I, too," said Father Grikos. "Give your father my best. I must speak to him soon about drugs. Tell him that. He'll understand. Now go with the good."

Actually it was Father Grikos who left first for Ktima—which Eleni thought of as "the city." With his robes held high, he went in a fury of haste, his long birdlike legs flashing through the dust, his umbrella over his shoulder like a rifle. A farmer touched his brow at the passage of the holy man. The priest never stopped. Eleni thought, "The English soldier was wrong. He is not a serpent in paradise. He is a vulture with a terrible beak." She, too, took to the road, in the opposite direction, toward New Paphos. Only the paintings were left, the blue Acropolis and the shield of Achilles covered with its cities and its fighting men.

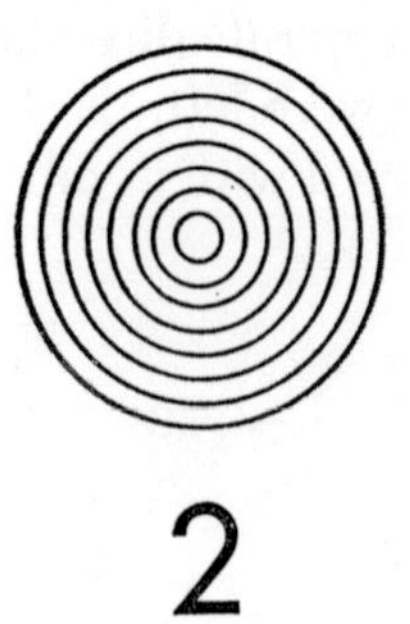

2

Eleni walked down the dusty road toward the sea. Mules, laden with concrete, bricks, and dusty sacks of cement, passed her on the road. A sizzling cloud of flies enveloped them, while above all in the blistering heat rose the delirium of the cicadas. When she got there, she would wade ankle-deep in the sea.

Here the walls were broken down, the fields stony, as though the sky had let fall some mysterious ruin. On the lower reaches of the road, vines spilled over crumbling walls. Fig trees of great age reared their muscular limbs, and their leaves were silver with dust. Here were carobs, too, and Eleni remembered that when a carob tree is slashed its wound is the color of human flesh.

Where the first houses began, Eleni passed her father's shop. She had no intention of conveying the priest's message. She passed quickly, her gaze boring into the ground.

Her earliest memories of her father were of a stocky soldier who had returned from the great war with a pocketful of medals. For a long time he had remained a hero, until a revelation had come from his own lips. Not only had he failed to win the medals as his celebrated brother in Athens had; he had panicked and run away. When Eleni refused to believe it he took the copper disks from their tissue paper, saying, "Look, they're Italian. I found them. I didn't win them. . . . Eleni, I'm only a small shopkeeper."

His pharmacy was in fact the largest in New Paphos and might have been extremely successful except for its location on the edge of the Turkish quarter. His customers had always been largely Turkish, but in the present political circumstances Lazarus dared not trade openly with them. Instead he saved his family from bankruptcy by conducting business through the back door at night.

Eleni's love for her father was not diminished by his failure as a soldier, or by his clandestine traffic with the Turks, whom Father Grikos considered mortal enemies. He had committed one unforgivable act, however, in which she felt herself a guilty partner. When her mother had become ill, they had sent her away. For her own good, for a cure, they had all agreed, but deep inside Eleni felt it was because her father was kept awake by the coughing at night, because she herself was afraid of a disease which, like an evil magician, had turned her young mother so suddenly into an old woman. For this reason, she could not talk to her father of important things as she once had. Raphael had become the one person to whom she could tell everything, and though he often laughed at her he somehow helped fill the hollowness that was more and more a part of her life.

She wanted to pass quickly through the Turkish quarter,

but with dignity, as one who carries a vessel of water on her head. "Go smilingly" was the traditional Turkish salute, but she seldom heard it any more. There were only the eyes, like gemstones set in blocks of flint. Turkish men wore wine-red fezzes. Turkish men wore beaded slippers and hammered out copper utensils with an awful din. Their young women were pretty, with large wet eyes, until black-toothed age turned them into bats huddled in doorways. Now nobody greeted her as she went by, except for a gaunt pariah dog that barked with surprise. Then all the bone-chewing, daydreaming alley dogs began to bark. She wanted to run. Deliberately she had to command each slow step.

Opposite the police station, where a commando stood on guard, she took a slow breath. However much she wanted to despise the English, the sentinel seemed a small island of security, and beyond him was Greek territory again. There the walls were roughly scrawled with EOKA signs. Even the Church of the Shrouded Madonna was disfigured with the familiar hieroglyphs and the scribbled dates of the last DDT sprayings. Finally came the stitched and cobbled ruin of the Byzantine castle, Saranta Kolones, where the Turkish children used to fly their colored kites. Beyond that was the breakwater, the gri-gris boats with their stern lanterns, the long nets drawn up for mending, and at last the sea. A row of fishermen sat along the breakwater baiting lines for trawling. Waves raced toward them, blue and fair, bursting white on the breakwater, filling the beach with a churning scrabble of pebbles sucked back in the undertow.

Eleni had no difficulty in finding Raphael. He worked apart from the other fishermen, a stranger to all the world, but she knew he was not lonely. A big awkward gargoyle of a boy, he rose when he saw her and started across the sand. His feet, swollen by salt water, were perpetually bare, and he rolled from side to side as he walked.

"*Yasu,*" he said, and stretched out his hand, a hand that was hard, with broad fingers and nails as tough as clamshells. But his eyes were soft, deep and dark and sparkling like the sea, with a terrifying sort of lucidity. Laughter slanted from his eyes, and he seemed about to smile. "Hey, you look worried. You're permitted to smile, to be of good cheer."

"It's nice here," she said.

"I like it better now you've come," he told her. She had no words for this, so she stared silently at the sea. "Come on over. I've got to get ready for tonight. We can talk while I work."

The fishing boat, like its owner, lived apart from the other boats in time as well as space. Old and weedy as the ark, such a hull might have been lying upon a reef, not floating upon the sea. It had been his father's boat, his grandfather's before that. The name so dimly implanted on the bow was *Nereid.* That bow was bearded with seaweed and barnacles, the deck scarred and worn like the hands of its owner.

"Sit down here," he told her, "out of the wind."

He held a basket of line and hooks between his legs and laid the hooks in a row around the rim. Between his toes he kept his spare needles and wax for mending the line.

"Go on, tell me," he said. "What's the matter?"

"I'm frightened. Did you hear the explosions?"

"No. The waves are too high. There must be a storm at sea."

The breakers thundered on the shore, and tiny sea gulls wheeled over the line of surf like fragments of blown spray.

"There were two explosions at Ktima," she explained. "Phaethon must have had something to do with them. The English are looking for him."

"So they're throwing bombs now. I was afraid . . ."

"I didn't say he threw any bombs. Oh, Raphael, if you

could have seen his face!" Remembering, Eleni involuntarily raised her hand to her cheek as if to shape the expression of her own face. "He was so frightened."

"And that's all you know?"

"I can't tell you more than there is to tell."

"Well, it's not the end of the world." His voice was beautiful, calm, as though isolated from emotion. "You know, they make those bombs out of water pipes. You have to be very clever not to blow off your fingers."

Raphael began to feed a fire under a pot of tar. Small waves lapped the shore at their feet and hissed away into the sand.

"Do you never think of anyone except yourself, Raphael?"

"Who else should I think of? I look after my job. Other things take care of themselves. When it comes to politics, I haven't any passion. I'm neutral."

"Everybody takes sides," she protested.

"All right, I'm on the side of life and a good time. I stay as I am."

"Sometimes to stand still is to change."

"You know, when people can't stand things as they are, they have a choice. They can become hermits, or they can make bombs. The second is Phaethon. But I'm not interested in politics." Mulishly, it seemed to Eleni, he repeated the sentiment.

"All right, but what about your friends? Neutrals are dangerous to know these days."

"I haven't got so many friends. Besides, I'm a coward. You can't turn me into a hero. At most, I could throw a book."

"That isn't funny," she said.

"No. I wish it were. I'm doing a bad job of cheering you up. You're in love with Phaethon, aren't you?"

"I guess so."

"Well, he used to be my best friend. I'm glad it's Phaethon. Would you call him a handsome devil?"

"He's very attractive," she said. Two tiny circles of color appeared briefly on her cheeks where the olive skin was tightly stretched over her cheekbones.

"Romantic, daring," said Raphael, "and 'come already into his hour,' as the Maltese would say."

She looked for motive in his face and saw nothing but friendliness.

"Have you never loved anyone?" she asked.

"Oh, the sea, and my father. They were pretty much alike."

Raphael was a strange one; so detached, with the cool air of one who had avoided all human involvement. Once she had felt in his wrist for a pulse. She'd found no heartbeat at all, and, laughing, he'd told her there wasn't any blood in his veins, only sea water. Sometimes it seemed almost true.

A strident whistle jarred her thoughts. Near the old castle an English soldier stood, his cheeks puffed out like the pictures of Aeolus. Presently other soldiers in bathing trunks and towels jogged around the breakwater. An old fisherman sucking wine from a blue enamel can watched them go.

"To think they'll be hunting Phaethon!" said Eleni. "All those men!"

"They'd rather go on swimming," said Raphael.

"I know. He used to play right here. All of us. Was that really so long ago?"

The cry of the gulls was clear and shrill. Waves washed up the beach, and with them memories, like echoes in a sea shell.

"We were good friends in those days, the three of us," she said. There had been a joy about them as they played on the beach. "You were like brothers, you and Phaethon."

"I think we were closer than brothers."

"And I was a scabby-kneed little brat with a voice like a parrot."

"I don't see much of Phaethon now, but I can't change even if he has," said Raphael.

Eleni said, "I remember the first time I saw you. I was in your father's boat, the one with the glass bottom."

"Yes, I remember."

"And you were underwater, fishing, with that helmet on your head and the bubbles coming up. I remember you had an octopus on a kind of pitchfork."

"A trident. I still use it for fishing."

"It was all slimy, the octopus. I thought you were brave, and I asked your name."

"I said I was a fisherman."

"And I said, 'What kind of a name is that?' . . . Funny, not having a last name."

"Remember," said Raphael, "those boats I used to make out of cigarette boxes with the pine-chip sails?"

"And my glass-bottle dolls I fed through the neck to see them digest?"

"But mostly we went swimming."

"You were the best," she said. "You knew how to dive. Phaethon used to jump in, feet first, stiff as a poker. I think he was really like me, scared to death of the water . . . I still am."

"Phaethon's funny. He always did the things that frightened him. If it hadn't frightened him, I don't think he'd have bothered with swimming. What a rotten swimmer! Just like a big muskrat, with only his eyes and nose sticking out. Once he practically drowned."

"That was my fault," said Eleni. "How awful, the way I made you two compete. You always won at swimming. And the time I got you both to eat fish—raw. Do you remember that?"

"Sometimes I still eat them that way," said Raphael. "Not fish, but shellfish."

"Oh, how angry Phaethon used to get, though, when you beat him. He was either in a rage or very gentle." Eleni recalled a day when the two boys had fought. Raphael had won a swimming match, and Phaethon had rushed at him with a rock in each hand, armed like a Stone Age savage. Raphael had the longer reach and the heavier fist. He had held out his arm more in self-defense than anything else, and Phaethon had blackened his eye on the end of it. They had made up afterward. Phaethon had even worn the eye as a kind of medal, but it seemed to Eleni that their relationship had never been quite the same again.

Jamal had arrived in Paphos about this time. He was no fighter, but a natural swimmer and an enthusiastic sailor. For these qualities Phaethon must have disliked him from the start, though to Eleni he simply said he hated all Turks.

Raphael said, "Phaethon wouldn't have gotten in those moods if it hadn't been for his father. He was always waiting to straighten Phaethon out. He's still waiting."

"Your father was more of a father to him than his own ever was," Eleni said.

"But my father killed himself, and we all grew up. And here we are."

"What went wrong, Raphael? Was it because you fought?"

"Boys always fight."

"Jamal, then?"

"*Hahm-dah Lil-lah*—It's the will of Allah," Raphael said.

"I think something must have started in school."

"It started there," said Raphael.

Eleni remembered the early days of unrest. Greek Cypriotes had always talked of union with Greece. They had hoped the British would go. Parents, priests, schoolteachers, all talked of it, and then one day the blackboard had been shrouded with crepe and the legend on it read, "We demand our freedom." The students had all signed a petition for Enosis, for union with Greece. It had been great fun. Later the signs had changed. "Enosis—Death to Armitage—The British Must Go." As a joke, Phaethon had written on the board, "Death to Everyone." They had not been in the school room any more but in the streets, chanting "E-E-Enosis, Ma-ka-ri-os," and "E-O-Ka." The girls had pelted the Turkish police with soda bottles. They had rioted in Ktima and New Paphos, and then had gone back to pass their school examinations. It was about this time, too, that Father Grikos had hounded Raphael out of school for having Turkish friends and for not supporting the petition. It hadn't mattered much, for soon the schools had closed. There remained only the rioting, the first bombs, and Dighenis.

Eleni had once, at a distance, seen Dighenis driving through town. He wasn't an impressive man, but little and wiry, with rotting teeth and the wild bright eyes of a chipmunk. But from the first they had called him Leader, and he had come to cast a mighty shadow. Gunmen had flocked to him, a terrorist army of liberation. Raphael had retired to the sea, but Phaethon had joined the Pan-Cyprian national youth organization. He had carried a sign: "Greeks, Liberty Is Won with Blood." Finally he had joined EOKA. He had become the Leader's man.

Eleni said, "Phaethon thinks Dighenis is a savior, that he'll drive the British out of Cyprus."

"He reminds me of one of those hard black bugs that sting," Raphael replied. "You squash it to pieces, but it goes on stinging and stinging just the same."

"You wouldn't say that if you cared what happened to Cyprus," she told him.

"Do you know what a desperado is? It's a man without

belief. He is guided only by a wild rage," said Raphael.

"The Leader isn't like that. Neither is Phaethon. They're both of them heroes."

"Well, there isn't anything worse than a determined hero. They say Agamemnon made mincemeat of his only daughter so Zeus would give him permission to start the Trojan War. Now even Zeus is dead, and Phaethon's still fighting the war."

"Shut up, Raphael. They may put Phaethon in jail."

"And after he has ripped out all the plumbing, they will hang him."

"Hang him!"

"I don't mean that. Phaethon knows this island. He won't be caught."

"But will they hang him if they catch him?"

"Probably, for throwing a bomb."

"He didn't say he threw it."

"But you believe he did. I don't know. I can't look into other men's souls and I can't condemn them, but somehow Phaethon always seemed too eager to take up arms and hunt his neighbors."

"That isn't fair, Raphael, and it isn't kind. Here you are, saying awful things about Phaethon while you go around fraternizing with the enemy."

"The enemy?"

"I mean Jamal."

Before the Turkish problem, she had been friendly with Jamal. His father had worked at the pharmacy, until the troubles. Jamal's father had been the hero her father had always failed to be. Captured in the great retreat from Monastir, he had escaped to Lesbos by raft with a bayonet, a wool cape he slept under at night, and little else but courage. If the young people coaxed him, he would describe how the pipers played at El Alamein. More than his quiet tales of glory, Eleni remembered his yellow kid boots and the way he used to paint the shop in salmon red with aquamarine stripes on the door.

"Why should it matter that he's a Turk? I like him," said Raphael.

She liked Jamal, too. He was like his father, a quiet man in a chattering world, his hands tranquil in a gesturing community. But his blood was Turkish blood; one couldn't change that.

"Has anyone ever told you that in Mohammed's tomb there's an empty chamber waiting for the body of Jesus?" asked Raphael. "No Moslem feels anything but respect and love for your Christian god. One day when the mountains erode and there's one universal sea, then all the gods will be one god."

"And Jamal's great-great-grandfather, or somebody, was Lala Mustafa. They stole Cyprus."

"Five hundred years ago. You might as well blame Cain for throwing stones."

"All right, but you're not doing Cyprus much good sitting here on this beach baiting hooks."

"I'm tarring my boat."

"You aren't doing yourself much good, either."

"I suppose you mean I'm not making money. I don't need a big mahogany desk to prop me up. What's money for? A half crown has always seemed just the right size to skip on the water. And I've never had much taste for digging mule dung up and down some devil's patch of a field."

"You don't show any concern for your future, Raphael."

"I suppose not," he said. Eleni raged inwardly because he refused to fight back.

"Everyone has to make plans, depend on something," she said. "What do you depend on?"

"I've told you. The sea. I don't know much about philosophy or religion, but the sea's my great blue god. I trust him."

Most people thought of the sea as a woman, but Raphael did not and neither did she. Eleni was afraid of the sea.

"I thought you came here for sympathy," said Raphael, "not to pick a quarrel."

"Have I gotten any?" Then she felt guilty. "Sorry, I'm not having a very good day today. Besides, I came to ask a favor. A big one." Raphael made no answer. "I'm going to meet Phaethon tonight. I have to take him things. Don't you want to know where he is?"

"No . . . yes, but I don't want to ask."

"It's the old tomb, where we used to play."

"And what's the favor?"

"I want you to go with me."

She could not see the expression on Raphael's face at first and did not know how he was reacting.

"You don't have to," she added quickly.

He turned to her, eyes brooding and kind. His mouth smiled a little without changing his eyes at all. "Have I ever not done what you asked?" he said. "Of course I'll go."

On the strength of his unfailing support, the sun seemed to brighten. A shy warm feeling of gratitude suffused her like a blush.

"If I were in charge of the ark," she said, "you'd be the first one I'd invite aboard."

"Don't you mean the second?" He allowed her no time for embarrassment. "Listen, do me a favor too. Come to Limassol for the wine festival."

"Limassol!"

"We'll sail down. It's a good day's sail, and you've got relatives there. I can sleep on the boat." Wrinkles of good nature radiated from the corners of his eyes. "What do you say?"

"I can't. Not while Phaethon needs help."

"I mean after."

"You know I'm afraid of the sea. There are storms this time of year."

"So I'll trace a pentagram on the mast and say the holy words. Nothing's sunk the *Nereid* in over sixty years. It'll do you good."

"I can't. I have to see Mother."

"At Chrysorroyiatissa?"

"Yes."

"Your mother's a great woman. I can see her up there with those monks, just like a dethroned empress. . . . How is she?"

"Helpless and awfully sick."

"Your mother? She's tough as a boot. She'll go right on along after you've rattled your engine to pieces."

"I wish I believed that. Anyway, I've got to see her before I leave for Athens." Truthfully, she had little desire to visit her mother. She did not know how to deal with illness and frailty, especially in her mother, who had once seemed as healthy as a keen-edged saber. For the past six months she had lived at the health resort run by the monks of Chrysorroyiatissa Monastery. She had tuberculosis, and it was through the intervention of Father Grikos that she was at the monastery. Although EOKA opposed any dealings with the British, the priest had obtained a welfare authorization when the village muhktar was afraid to issue it.

All along he had taken charge of the illness. At first he had referred Demeter to various island saints for a cure. She had journeyed to the wonder-working image of Kykko, to the cross of the penitent thief at Stavrovouni, to the dry well where the bones of Saint Barnabas had been found; but the long trips on the dusty roads had only aggravated her condition. Finally Father Grikos had resorted to the

English medical authorities, had obtained the authorization, and the progress of the disease had been checked. But he could just as readily rescind the authorization, which was the real reason Eleni could not go to Limassol with Raphael.

"When is it you leave for Athens?" he asked.

"As soon as I get back from the monastery. In about a week."

"So a boy escapes to the sea, and a girl to Athens."

That was true, in her case. She would be escaping her mother's sickness and her father's worry. It made her feel guilty to think so.

"Are you scared of what it's going to be like?" he asked.

"No," she said quickly, "no, I'm not. You've been there, haven't you?"

"I stopped by Piraeus."

"Not the Acropolis?"

"No, I was just a few hours in Piraeus. I've been to Naples, Barcelona, Alexandria, too." He named them painstakingly, the cities beyond the main.

"Sea gypsy," said Eleni. "You don't have to brag."

"How long will you be gone?"

"Till summer. The end of the term."

"It's really something to win an art scholarship like that. 'For the most promising young artist in Cyprus,' that's what the letter said, didn't it? I envy you."

"I know better. You don't envy me at all."

"I suppose you're right," he admitted. "I don't really envy anyone."

In fact, it was the other way around. Eleni envied him his guileless joy in life. "If you were a god, wouldn't you change anything?" she asked.

"Yes. I'd have my father alive again."

"Not your mother?"

"I hardly remember her. But I can still see my father."

So could Eleni; lean, dark, his garments bedizened with talismans from the sea: shells for buttons, sea-bird feathers in his cap, and his shirt open, showing a broad hairy chest. He had played a concertina, and his hair had been blue-black like Raphael's hair, and wavy like the sea.

"People just used to call him 'the Maltese,'" said Raphael. "Nobody knew his real name, just 'the Maltese,' but he called himself a disinherited son of the sea. He said he had been cast up here like a tree trunk. My grandfather was a real seaman, you know. He sailed around both capes in a square-rigged ship. It was his concertina my father played. Now it belongs to me."

"If your father loved the sea so much, why did he settle down?"

"Because he married my mother here. He said she was a sea nymph that had enchanted him. Her eyes were so good to live in, he couldn't leave, so he shouldered his oar and took to the land. To the beach, anyway. When he went out fishing, she went along; but she got sick, you know, and died one night of pneumonia while he scolded her for coughing. They say in death she looked like a wise child. I wasn't allowed to see her. I was too young. My father and I fished together alone after that. He was never the same. He used to tell me that a man should never fall in love, and that he belonged to the sea. He called it the cradle of life, and I guess he couldn't stand things the way they were."

"That's when he rowed out in the glass-bottom boat," said Eleni.

"And they found the boat wrecked next day."

"They never found him, did they?" she asked.

"No. I don't think he meant to drown himself. Maybe he didn't die at all. He was more fish than man anyway. Maybe he found those deep caverns where the mermaids live, all strewn with pearls and fine coral. He told me once he saw a mermaid on a stormy night. He wasn't sure whether her hair was green or gold, but her eyes were the color of moonlight. Funny, even now I can't imagine him drowned, like a dead dog, all bloated on the beach. Whenever I'm sailing alone, I feel him there with me. I don't see him but I can hear him whisper. It's hard to explain, but that's why I am the way I am, you know, private."

"Irresponsible, you mean."

"That's part of it. You have to use words when you tell about the sea, but words aren't good enough for the feel of a good boat spanking along and all the horizons calling out loud."

Eleni could feel that call now, but only from one horizon, in the west, beyond which lay Athens. She longed for the day of departure.

"When I get ready to die," he said, "I hope I can do it like my father. Just disappear into the sea."

"Don't talk about dying," she told him, and then she remembered that Phaethon, too, had talked of death. He wanted to be buried in one of the ancient tombs, the one where she would meet him tonight.

With the midafternoon had come the meltemi wind, bringing a breath of coolness from the sea. It carried the waves a little farther up the beach, and with the waves came tiny transparent creatures to scavenge briefly on the sand. Eleni clasped her arms about her. She felt cold from the wind and from thinking of the sea; it was so deep and mysterious.

Raphael had begun tarring the *Nereid.* There was tar two inches thick and fifty years old on the ancient boat, but he tarred again with a long brush. He threw more sticks on the fire under the tar pot. One of the larger sticks must have contained a nest, for in the heat it began to swarm with ants. Impulsively, Eleni reached for the stick, but the fire was too hot. She drew back.

Raphael shrugged. *"Hahm-dah Lil-lah,"* he said, but her concern for the ants must have shown in her face. "All right, for you I'll play God a little," and without even seeming to hurry, he put his hand into the fire, took hold of the stick, and placed it on the sand. Eleni cried out at this strangely moving gesture, almost a ritual sacrifice.

"Oh, your hand, your poor hand . . ." and she would have taken his hand in both of hers but she could not bear to look at the burns.

"I didn't feel it," he said.

"You're crazy!" she told him. "You're really out of your mind," but she felt a rush of happiness.

"I know it," he admitted.

"Right in the hollow of your left ear there's some fine sand, like in a shell," she told him, and with a finger she brushed the sand away. "There."

Both were smiling, with the same innocent pleasure, self-forgetful, fond, and foolish, when the English bathers jogged back onto the beach. They rushed shouting for the sea and tumbled into the waves. There were girls with them now and the girls tucked up their skirts and waded out ankle-deep.

When Eleni saw the soldiers, she imagined Phaethon cowering in darkness, dreading their approach. This unhappy picture was banished by the arrival of the Turk, Jamal. He had almost reached her before she was aware of him; a small dark figure clad in dusty black, a green cloth band binding back his long dark hair. He advanced with a lively stride. His vitality was the most striking thing about him. Even in his ragged clothing, it did not seem possible that any seed of decay or sickness could exist amid such glowing health. Jamal looked immortal.

"Health, Raphael," he called.

"Health to you. Sit down, Jamal, join us. You know Eleni."

They greeted one another with embarrassed formality. His smile, she thought, was a Turkish smile, wanting to please and not knowing how. It bothered her to see him act that way. If only he were confident, hard. "Well, I've been here too long already. I've got to be running." She sounded like a liar and her "It was nice seeing you again, Jamal," provided no redemption.

"Eleni . . ." With his voice, with a single word, he seemed to be trying to hold her, but time had eroded a great chasm between them. "Eleni . . ."

"Yes?" she said, in a tone that was not helpful.

"Eleni, do you still have those glass dolls? The ones you used to feed?"

"They were nothing but bottles," she told him. "They've all been broken and thrown out."

"Remember the time they had indigestion and I was whipped for stealing aspirin from the store?" She returned a faint smile of acknowledgment. "My father sends his best to your father. He looks forward to better times."

"Yes, I'll tell Father." Didn't they all look forward to better times? But better times for a Greek could never mean better times for a Turk as well, at least not in Cyprus. "I really have to go. I'll see you tonight, Raphael."

"Until tonight," echoed Raphael, and he sounded disappointed. In her? How could he expect her to fraternize with a Turk while her family was in such an awkward position? If she hadn't been tactful, that was too bad. She wasn't sorry, she told herself, and this too was a lie.

From the breakwater she looked back. The two young men were busy loading the boat. The work was heavy, but they toiled with the rhythm of those who work for themselves. Over the waves she thought she heard them singing, well-matched voices in the rapport of close friendship.

Then Raphael went down to the water's edge. He knelt and put his hand in the water and held it there, the one that had borne the burning stick. Farther down the beach, British soldiers played, and where the boulders stood up in the surf the hard salt glittered on the harder stone.

Eleni took the long way home, avoiding the Turkish quarter entirely. She was almost there when she met Father Grikos. He stood in the road blocking the path as though he had been waiting. They walked the rest of the way together, his lank body swinging along so briskly that she had to execute a few light skips to keep up.

"Did you go to Ktima?" she asked.

He had, but he wasn't volunteering any information.

"Was it a bomb?"

It was.

"And was anyone killed?"

Here he began to talk. A bomb had been thrown into a jeep. An English soldier had been killed, another injured. So it had really come to bombs at last. There had been bombs before, in Nicosia, and she knew the archbishop had sent out his permission long ago. But never here in Paphos. There was no sport in bombing. It wasn't like throwing soda bottles at the old-fashioned riot shields of the Turkish police. You didn't just go back to school after throwing a bomb.

She wanted to ask about Phaethon, but there was no interrupting Father Grikos now. His eyes rolled up to the sky and his voice rich in pulpit tones, he seemed to be preparing a sermon. "EOKA is a gift from God," he intoned. "Once in a generation, people are ready to rise above material things. Our people are ready now, with heroes like your Phaethon to lead them."

Father Grikos had stopped in the middle of the road. His long pale face glowed with the great vision. "Rising up in the red dawn came Christ the tiger," he exclaimed, and Eleni took one hesitant step back. Was she in the presence of a mystic? Then just as suddenly he laughed, seized her arm, and pulled her along. "This is a great day," he said. "A great and glorious day."

"Please tell me everything that happened. What about Phaethon? And Stephan?"

"Stephanides Diakos will be our first martyr," he told her. "He has killed an Englishman in cold blood, and they will hang him."

"Mother of God!"

"Remember, my dear, we live in a land where martyrdom is a tradition. Here in Paphos, Paul was scourged by the Romans. There have been many martyrs since, and your friend Stephanides will not be the last." A martyr. Stephan was a martyr now and this knowledge seemed to soften, even lend a certain beauty, to a face she had always regarded as ugly, almost bestial.

"These English! They try to pacify us with a constitution fit for Fuzzy-Wuzzies. Never! The road to any compromise will be piled high with bodies." In the monk's voice she seemed to hear the genuine accents of prophecy. Were not there less bloody ways to achieve union with Greece? A quotation from the Bible came to her lips, but she held her tongue. It would be blasphemy to encroach upon the priest's domain.

"How is the master of the house?" said Father Grikos. "Did you give him my message?"

"Of course," she lied.

"And how did he react?"

"He said he was looking forward to seeing you."

Father Grikos watched her with a look that was not quite definable. Was he amused? Annoyed? She felt like a bug being scorched under a magnifying glass.

"How's his business?"

"Well, you know, times are hard."

Father Grikos thrust his face close to hers and his terrible eyes seemed to penetrate her soul. "You're lying like Ananias," he told her, calm and affable. He was not going to be duped.

Little drops of perspiration appeared on her upper lip. She felt her temples tighten under the stress of dishonesty.

"Listen to me now, Eleni. I have spoken to you before about visiting that excommunicant, and yet you will not listen. You have no idea the hours I labored with that boy to help him see the light. He's incorrigible. He deserts his own people in their hour of travail. He consorts with pagans. You talk to him of God and he laughs in your face. You talk to him of the devil and he still laughs. His is the greatest sin, Eleni: spiritual pride. The sin of Lucifer!"

"You don't understand him. He's his own worst enemy."

"Not while I'm alive," said Father Grikos.

"Truly. He only wants to be let alone. He means no harm."

"He's sold his soul to the devil. That's harm enough."

"Why should the devil be buying souls? He can get all he wants for nothing."

"That's clever," said the priest. He moved his eyelids in his version of a smile. "Do you know that girls with impudent thoughts break out in pimples?"

Her fists tightened at her sides.

In rich, unctuous tones he seemed tirelessly ready to instruct. "You're an exceptional young person," he began, "but just remember, few people have had your advantages."

What might have been a long and agonizing lecture ended abruptly with the honking, dust-whirling passage of a lorry full of English soldiers returning to barracks. Raising arms wide like black wings, Father Grikos shouted after them, "Generation of serpents!" Then to Eleni, "They spit in our faces and we have to say it's raining. But Paphos is three thousand years old. All its conquerors have gone back to ashes. Well, I must go. This awful dust!" He waved at the thick air.

"Wait. . . . You haven't told me about Phaethon. The second bomb . . ."

"Well, he's all right. You saw him get away."

"Did he throw the second bomb?"

Father Grikos gave a churchyard cough. "Honestly, my dear, I don't know who discharged the second bomb. It wasn't actually thrown. It was dropped in a mailbox, right beside the New Palace Hotel."

"Go on."

"Apparently it didn't go off right away. A little girl was passing when the box exploded . . ." Eleni felt as if two red thumbs were pressing on her eyeballs. "No, my dear, it wasn't that bad. She wasn't killed. The English have taken her away in an ambulance. She may only lose a hand, if she's lucky. Sometimes it is very difficult to see God's purpose, but I know well there is one. He never makes a mistake. The Lord giveth—are you all right, my dear? Can I help you?"

"I have to go home," she told him through clenched teeth.

"Then go, my dear. May God keep you in the hollow of His hand." But she wanted nothing of God's hands. She wanted to be alone.

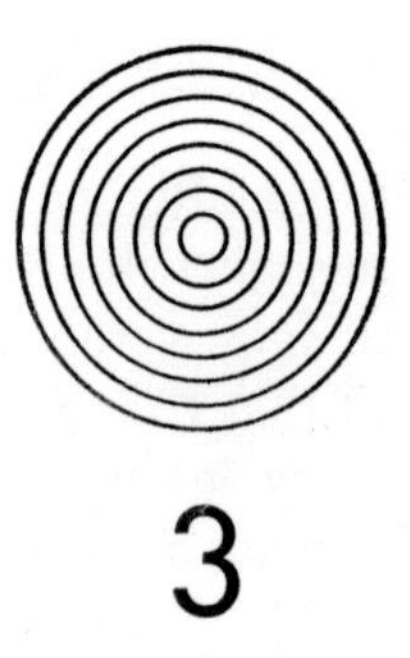

3

A brace of goat's horns hung over the doorway to prevent the evil eye from entering. Eleni passed under them without looking up. Her father's store was like a gloomy cavern, cluttered to the ceiling with drugs and herbs. On the right were the old, sometimes magical remedies in jars and tiny cloth bags. To the left, sealed in plastic and glass, were the drugs from Europe and America. She sniffed among them for the seminal smells of mice and rats, then passed toward the rear where sugary Cyprus brandy and kegs of Othello wine lined the shelves. Her father's domain was in the rear, separated by a bead curtain from the rest of the shop. Here he kept a bed, a chair, and a small charcoal stove. The chair and the stove had always been there; the bed only since her mother's illness, though lately he had slept at home.

Eleni parted the curtain and entered. Lazarus Lambros lay on the bed, his hands clasped above his head. He wore his habitual black coat and faded khaki pants, the remains of a World War II uniform. In the street he would wear black shoes, highly polished, but here he enjoyed the comfort of Turkish slippers. He gave the appearance of a quiet, solid man, worthy of respect. A man of malleable iron, he called himself.

Their greeting was an exchange of grunts.

Eleni put down her bag of food, which contained supper and enough to feed Phaethon for two days. She began to stir up the charcoal in the small stove and when it was hot placed six big fresh silvery sardines in a black pan.

Her father uncorked a bottle of retsina wine and poured it into two tin cups. He lit a stub of candle because the light was fading, but neither of them had really spoken by the time the sardines were done.

Eleni put the sardines on two plates and set them on the small table. Her father was already seated. He hunched over his food, and his tiny circumflex of a mustache moved with the motion of his jaws. The sardines vanished. Bread was broken to mop up the olive oil, and still there was no conversation. Eleni expected none, for they rarely had anything to say to one another.

Eleni cleared the plates away while her father pulled a tobacco pouch from his belt and rolled a cigarette.

"Those things make you cough," she told him.

He did not answer, but from the way he cleared his throat and adjusted his collar, she guessed they were in for one of their rare conversations.

"Eleni . . ."

"Yes?" She scraped the plates loudly.

"Eleni . . . look at me. I want to tell you something."
She put the plates into the rusty sink.
"Do you remember I used to have a Turkish employee? Remember Sabri? We worked well together. We were very good friends, but I had to let him go." Her father's voice was oddly shy; there was a cough lurking behind it. "You know why that was?"
"Tell me, Father," she said, though she knew perfectly well.
Lazarus fumbled in his pocket, where he kept little bundles of things: cards, lists, a small calendar, all held together by rubber bands. He found a match and lit his cigarette.
"Eleni, the world's out of joint. You and I aren't the ones to force it back into shape. We're Greek. That's why I let my mustache grow, to look more Greek. It's not patriotism, but everyone pulls the quilt to his side of the bed. If I hadn't fired Sabri, Father Grikos would not have told his congregation to come here for remedies. He's been here to see me this afternoon. He was rather upset—about you."
So that was it. You could trust Father Grikos not to overlook an awkward situation.
"You upset him very much," Lazarus continued.
"I didn't mean to do anything like that."
"Well, you did. You know that now, don't you?"
No reply.
"I say, you know that, don't you, Eleni?"
"Yes. I'm sorry, Father, if I make it difficult for you."
Lazarus blew out a long stream of smoke. The crickets in the crannies fretted the silence. "The devil take him for interfering. I like that boy, Raphael—but we're like some kind of unholy trinity: Greeks, Turks, English. I'd take a chance and say go ahead, keep your old friends—but Eleni, there's your mother—Demeter." He spoke her name sadly,

with the air of a man who explains an insoluble situation in a single word. "Father Grikos has the power of life and death over her."

Eleni knew this was true. The medical certificate hung like a sword of Damocles above them all.

"He said good things about you too. He told me about Phaethon and how you intend to help him with food. Is it in that bag?"

Eleni nodded.

"I can't deny he's a worthy lad. Headstrong, but he'll make a good husband one day." Not long ago Eleni remembered her father discussing Phaethon in other terms. He had predicted the boy would find himself sitting in a dungeon without a key, but that was before it was dangerous to criticize EOKA. "When his father dies and they pry him open, all sorts of gold and jewels will fall out. Phaethon'll be a wealthy young man. You don't know what it's like, being old and as poor as Job's goat."

Eleni had been regarding her father with a steady grimace of annoyance. He must have noticed this, for again he introduced the unopposable argument. "With such wealth, think what you can do for your mother. Even the great hospitals of Switzerland."

"Father, you won't like this, but I'm going to tell you anyway. When I saw Raphael this afternoon, I asked him to go along."

"Tonight?" His hands rose and fell in a slack gesture of helplessness. "As long as that priest doesn't find out! Raphael's a fine young man, too, like his father. I will always owe his father a great debt."

Eleni knew he meant the time at Kalamata, when the German dive bombers had come down over the faded red tile roofs and bombed the beaten armies of England and Greece as they tried to hide among the flowering almond trees. Most of the British troops had gotten off to the destroyers, but not many of the Cypriotes had escaped. Most of them had been killed or captured. In that last desperate day a familiar fishing boat had appeared, its sails riddled with bullets, and Lazarus had been saved, along with as many Cypriotes as the boat would hold. All this Eleni had heard before, and she felt a faint sickness in her heart when she heard again of the dead companions of her father's youth.

"I'm going now, Father," she told him.

He took both her hands. "I don't like you doing these dangerous things. Thank God you'll be going to Athens soon."

"You don't know what's going on," she said. "Some of the other girls have guns."

"I don't want you involved that way. Just this once—" His hands loosened. They slipped lifelessly to his sides. "I don't know what the world's coming to," he added softly.

"Turn on the wireless and you'll find out."

"I'm sick of the news," he said, but he flicked the knob of the small portable radio and a voice from Athens shouted with unexpected vigor, "Enosis, and only Enosis . . ."

Lazarus stretched out on the bed, his shirt open, his arms again under his head. He did not smoke or speak. He just lay there, looking at the ceiling, listening to the radio. Eleni could not help thinking, "My father, he's only a small shopkeeper. He'll lie there all evening waiting for the Turks to come and kick off their shoes and creep through the back door. When there are no more customers, he'll shut the door and sleep with his hands over his head because that was how he lay among the almond trees of Kalamata when the bombers came screaming down."

Out on the road, Eleni gathered her hair and tied it at the back of her neck with a black ribbon. She looked up and down for the priest, but the road by the chapel was empty.

Toward the Turkish quarter, women sat in the cobbled street making lace. Girls scrubbed doorsteps and filled flowerpots with water while the houses fell into shadow and the white minarets became rosy. High overhead, the buzzards swung in soaring circles.

Once again she took the long way, through the fields. She loved the fragrant smell of the red earth rising up with the evening, mixing with the sticky sweet fragrance of the carob trees. With a long-limbed stride she went, and wished she were not going. She would rather lie down here and hide, like a field mouse. As a child, she sometimes had hidden in the fields all day long, and once she'd been so still that a tiny green lizard had crawled very close to her ear. If he had spoken, as he had seemed about to do, his message would have changed the world. But the lizard did not speak. Yet she had felt his cold remote tongue against her ear, and thought the world a lovely friendly place.

Now the night was coming on and she had no time for lizards. Already the sky was hazy and purple. Gnats whirled up, silver against the last light. No men worked in the fields. Their weary voices rose in song from wine shops. Gradually these sounds were lost in the slow respirations of the sea.

Where the fields gave way to the beach and the sea, she paused. The sun lay on the water like a scarlet ball, and she felt that in just such an instant Aphrodite must have risen from the waves and chosen this island, this very beach, as her home. Then the sun was gone and she was conscious of evening as the end of warmth. Quite close to the water's edge a fire burned, and as she approached, it grew brighter, throwing what looked like a sheen of orange oil upon the ripples. Two men huddled near the blaze, and she heard over the waves the music of an accordion and a pleasant voice singing merrily and quite off-key.

Jamal saw her first, and rose. He smiled his embarrassed, shy smile, and she thought, "If it weren't for his pleated trousers and headband, how much he looks like a Greek."

"When the fire blazes high, it heralds an important visitor. We knew you were coming."

She smiled without replying and they both waited for Raphael to finish his song. But the singer was overcome with mirth and could not continue. "Ignore me. I sound like wind in an old sea shell." He laughed just as he sang, freely and without affectation. "Hungry?" he asked.

Even if she had been starving, Eleni would not have eaten ink fish and macaroni.

"I guess you'd like to get this business over with," he said.

"Yes, it makes me nervous."

"Nothing will happen," Raphael assured her. But what if something did? What if the British were there with their dogs and Sten guns? "All right, I'll eat later, then. Let's go."

"Go with the good," said Jamal. She wondered if this were irony.

Raphael led her along the beach. The sun had disappeared, but the moon was rising, its liquid light trickling down the bouldered shoreline, sparkling on the ripples.

It was said that youths came this way on such a night to anoint the stones of Aphrodite's temple with oil and almond water. No one seemed to be abroad tonight, and presently they turned away from the beach, going inland over rough ground. There were over a hundred ancient tombs here, many of them only open holes. It was a dangerous place to walk in at night, and they went slowly.

Raphael moved with a groping roll. His big feet splayed out as though he gripped the ground with his toes. As a child, he had never had proper shoes.

"He'll be in the big one with the Doric columns, won't he?" asked Raphael.

"Yes. That's where he used to hide from his father," she said.

"Then we have to cross the whole field."

As they drew nearer, Eleni's breathlessness embarrassed her. She was afraid Raphael might notice. "What an airless night it is."

"I hadn't noticed," he said. "Slow down, will you?" His voice, like his actions, seemed mild and unhurried, as though he were no more involved in this adventure than in singing a song.

"There it is," he said.

Before them rose the blue-black mouth of the palaeokastra, the burying place of an ancient king. On the threshold they paused.

"My mouth's so dry," she said.

Raphael held out his hand, palm upward. "Look," he said, "the moonlight overflows like honey. It's a beautiful night. Don't be afraid."

For a moment they stood close together, listening. "It's so bright I can see the moon reflected in your eyes," he said, and she could see the black clouds reflected in his. "Come on, we'll go in and call his name."

In her childhood, the tomb had seemed a cozy place, a fortress, always smelling as though it were raining outside. Tonight it smelled of bats. She had not gone five paces inside when she felt a third person in the chamber. Something rustled in the darkness. "Is that you?" she whispered. Pale and indistinct, Phaethon materialized before her like a vapor exhaled from the ground.

"Thank God, Eleni, it's you. But I thought I heard voices. I told you to come alone." Phaethon struck a match. His dark passionate face glowed in the fluttering light. Then he frowned. "Ah, I did hear voices. Raphael, it's been a long time." His voice was warm, but his face bore a hostile smile.

He turned back to Eleni. "You look fine, the only beautiful thing I've seen all day. Did you bring food?" She handed him the sack. "Good. You didn't by any chance find a gun? I didn't think so."

"Did you throw a bomb today?" she asked him.

"I had one. . . . I couldn't make myself throw it right in their faces."

She thought of the two explosions and asked, "Did Stephan carry more than one bomb?"

"How should I know?"

"Are you telling the truth? Phaethon, answer me!"

"I'm telling you what happened."

She wanted to believe him. She had no reason to doubt except that his voice sounded noncommittal, as though the words meant the opposite of what they said. Eleni bit her lips, a way of hers when she thought she was hearing a lie.

"You aren't still carrying a bomb around?" she asked. To be found with such a weapon could mean death in the English court.

"Lord, no. I got rid of it," he said. "I got rid of everything so I could run. I kept feeling those dogs tearing at my legs. I kept hearing them in the distance."

"There weren't any dogs. The soldiers came in a truck," said Eleni. At last she began to believe. He sounded so like a little boy terrified by a nightmare, and a nightmare is seldom deadly.

"Did they catch Stephan?" he asked.

Raphael nodded.

"Did they kill him?"

"No, he's in prison."

"He'll be hung!"

"That's the law. People were killed by the bombs."

Between each sentence spoken there had been an apprehensive silence, as though Phaethon's grenade were lodged among the words. Until Eleni had exactly located the explosive, disarmed it in her mind at least, she would not feel at ease. Again she asked him what he had done with his bomb. As though encouraged by the sound of his own voice, Phaethon proceeded to elaborate the events of the morning. The grenades had been homemade, their first attempt at ammunition manufacture, and neither boy had any idea whether they would explode. "Mine didn't," said Phaethon. "Stephan threw his grenade, but Holy Madonna! I was scared right down to the bottom of my guts. I couldn't get the fuse going, and I had to get rid of it . . . well, I posted it."

"What do you mean?" Eleni's voice was small and cold.

Phaethon laughed, a curious hissing sound. "I dropped it in a mailbox and ran."

Eleni's fingers pressed hard against her eyes as though to eradicate the tomb, Phaethon, all that had been said.

"Eleni, what's wrong with you?" said Phaethon, looking down at her with furious anxiety.

"It went off in the mailbox. Didn't you hear it?" said Raphael.

"No, it didn't go off!" shouted Phaethon.

"I'm sorry," said the fisherman. "It did some harm."

"You're lying!" But Eleni repeated the story as it had come from Father Grikos. Phaethon shook his head steadily, first in denial, then in gradual comprehension. He turned to the wall and pounded his fist against it repeatedly. At each blow he uttered a terrible groan as though he were painfully driving nails.

"Hush! Someone will hear. That's over. There's nothing we can do." Eleni was able to speak calmly because she had rehearsed so often during the afternoon. The truth that she had all along suspected was simply confirmed and she was able to accept it more quickly than Phaethon. Through inadvertence, fate, the fortunes of war, whatever she chose to call it, a child had been maimed. Such misfortunes were commonplace even in a good cause and one had to be sensible and consider the larger issues. Besides, it was a child she did not know.

"I was out of my mind."

"For a little while," she agreed. That was the best explanation. For a little while he had been insane. "You're all right now."

"Do you hate me?"

"Phaethon, you were risking your life to do a good thing. I love you."

He stood unmoving, slumped against the wall. Only his eyes seemed alive in the candlelight, and they were full of torment. They were so close to her own they seemed all one black pupil, dark and fearful as a deer's when it hears the thicket stir under the hunter's boot.

"Eleni, they'll hang me. I'm afraid. I've been afraid ever since I got into EOKA. Do you know what it's like to be sure without a shadow of a doubt that you'll be killed? Sooner or later. I ought to feel sorry for that little girl, but I just feel sorry for myself. At night I wake up shivering. I pray 'Holy Mother, get me out of this, Holy Mother, please get me out of this.' "

"You don't have to stay in EOKA," she assured him. "You can go back to forestry school. You'd be safe there. The term must start in a few days."

"They wouldn't take me back."

"Why?"

"That's another nasty story. It's no good, Eleni. I ought to be dead. I ought to crawl back with Menelaus, or Ajax, whoever's buried back there. What peace, to be two thousand years dead . . ." And for some time he kept his eyes closed as though he were dead. When he opened them again, they were different: brighter, more intent. "As long as you stick by me, I'll make it," he said.

"I'll do anything, you know that," she promised. "Come, sit down by me, rest."

Against their backs rose a column: Doric, Ionic, she wasn't sure. There were eight such columns obscured by the darkness, but she remembered them from childhood games—and a smaller chamber behind them for the sarcophagus.

For some time all three were silent. Eleni tried to recall the old games they had played here, when Phaethon had been king. Finally, when it did not seem that Phaethon was ever going to speak, she said, "Phaethon, we've plans to make." She meant plans for his safety, but apparently he understood her otherwise.

"As soon as this is over, we'll be married. That's a promise, and we'll go to the Fontana Amorosa together. Oh, Eleni, you'll bring me luck." To Raphael he said, "You know we'll be getting married."

"My blessing," said Raphael. "On both of you. May you live to be old and have many children."

"What's the matter with you two?" cried Eleni. "We've got to get Phaethon out of here. Listen, if I get in touch with your father, surely he can do something?"

"My father! The only thing he ever really loved is the British Empire. Wait till he hears what I did."

"But he's still your father."

"When I was small, he punished me with a slap in the face. Then I would have to kiss his hand. No, I've left my father's roof, and I'm not going back. Besides, there's something else. I'm in EOKA. I've taken an oath, and if I don't do as I'm told, I'll be killed."

"Is it that bad?"

"That bad. You don't know the district leader. When he makes a suggestion, you do it or"—here he made a magician's pass with his hand—"you disappear."

"You're being silly."

"I'm dead serious . . . dead. Do you suppose I'd have got into this if I'd known? I mean, it's one thing carrying signs. But bombs! If there was any way at all I'd get out, but there's no one to turn to except you and Raphael and the district leader. If I could get a message through to him in the mountains, he'd get me out of this. Raphael, could you . . ."

"Don't ask me," said Raphael sadly. "I intend to be neutral. I don't want to wake up one morning with a cartridge belt around my waist."

Phaethon looked angry. A muscle in his cheek moved as he stared down at his feet. "You've never cared what happened to Cyprus. You've never really cared for anything." The anger seemed wound up tight inside him like a steel spring. "Either that or you're a coward."

"That's it," said Raphael agreeably. "Not a coward at heart, but a coward in action. The heroes have a much better chance of getting killed."

"Raphael's amusing," said Phaethon, his voice full of sarcasm.

"I'd like to help you, Phaethon, but I can't."

"You mean you won't."

"I can't. I haven't a pass to get through the patrols. What would a fisherman be doing in the mountains? Be reasonable."

"You mean you won't," Phaethon repeated.

"All right. Have it your own way."

Phaethon spoke as though Eleni were the only person present. "He's a filthy bloodsucker that won't drop off when it's got a bellyful—and he knows it." Then to Raphael: "Are you or aren't you?" But Raphael ignored the provocation.

Eleni started to speak but Phaethon interrupted. "You're going to regret this."

"Perhaps," admitted Raphael. "I regret a great many things."

Phaethon took a step forward, his hand half closed as though clutching a large stone. No hatred could be that bitter unless it were mixed with love, and Eleni thought she saw both in Phaethon's face. Before she could intervene, he stopped himself. "It isn't your fault," he said. "You didn't get me into this. . . . I feel lousy and sick."

"You may be sick all right, but I wonder if you feel it," said Raphael.

Phaethon looked at him without anger. "No more, please. Don't you think I've damned myself more than you can ever do?"

Eleni caught hold of Phaethon's hand. "Stop it!" she said. "Both of you. Old friends hating one another when we ought to be making plans. Phaethon, tell me how, and I'll carry your message."

"I don't want that. You're a girl," said Phaethon, but his objection sounded more a matter of form than of conviction.

"All the more reason. I won't be searched. Besides, I have a pass to visit my mother at Chrysorroyiatissa."

"Chrysorroyiatissa! There's a pickup point right there." He spoke with joy, then became more subdued. "Still, I don't like it. It may be dangerous." His objections were easily overcome, and it was not until he had produced pencil and paper and had begun to write that Eleni considered the possible consequences. If she were caught, at the very least she would be sent to prison.

Raphael paced back and forth. Obviously he regretted coming, and Eleni pitied him. His embarrassment was her fault, but she couldn't help feeling that he had played the coward.

When the note was finished, Phaethon folded it carefully

and handed it to Eleni. She did not want to know its contents and slipped it unread into her blouse. "Listen carefully," he told her. "You know the ruined chapel? On the old altar, there's a stone. Slip this under the stone and it'll be found. That's all there is to it."

"I'll do it only if you both apologize. You're too good friends to go away despising each other."

At her bidding, the young men shook hands, a gesture without warmth or duration.

"I'm sorry," said Phaethon. "Honestly I am . . . I'm ashamed of myself. I swear that once I get out of this safely . . . well . . ." Phaethon gave the fisherman a comradely punch. "May you never die until I shoot you, and that's the wish of an old friend. You know that."

Once again his mood had changed. He was smiling and gay, far too gay for one whose conscience had been heavily burdened only moments before. It occurred to Eleni that Phaethon was a stranger whose emotions she completely failed to understand. "I don't know him," she thought with a kind of panic, and yet their futures seemed more bound together than ever before.

"We should go," said Raphael. "I want to get out before dawn."

"Eleni, you will take the message tomorrow?" asked Phaethon.

"If you promise to have nothing more to do with bombs."

"On my honor. I'll work for EOKA as hard as I can, but not that way." As Eleni turned to follow Raphael out of the tomb, Phaethon added, as though prompted by a demon, "Eleni, I must do what the Leader tells me," and thus casually deprived his promise of all value. Still, it was good to be outside again in the fresh air. She took a long cool breath and tried to put his final words from her mind.

As they walked, a light breeze sprang up. "It's late," she said.

"No, it's early. Soon the stars will dim."

"Once you told me the earth is swimming in stars."

"In Islam they say that every man has his own star which appears when he is born and goes out when he dies," said Raphael.

"I wonder which is mine," she said. "Is that one yours? The one over the sea?"

"It's far too bright to be mine."

All the stars were growing pale.

"Raphael," she asked, "why did you act such a sheep with Phaethon? Was he right? Are you really a coward?"

"I don't blow trumpets before the walls of Jericho—I can tell you that."

"I'm sorry I got you to go along."

"It doesn't matter."

"You don't like Phaethon any more, do you?" she said.

"I don't know him any more." That was an evasion. "I feel we're strangers. I think you and Phaethon are strangers, too."

Raphael and Phaethon had very little in common, it was true. Except for her, they would probably never see each other again. Yet to think of Phaethon as a stranger, however obscure his motivations, was impossible. If any one of them had to be the outsider, it must be Raphael.

As they returned along the beach, the long slow swell stretched into a motionless belt that fringed the southern shore of Cyprus. Where the ripples broke, phosphorescence glowed like green fire. Out on the sea the gri-gris boats could be identified by their cyclops eyes of light. They used conch shells for signaling, and they were coming in with a shuddering harvest of silvery scales and drumming fins.

"It will be a good morning for sailing," said Raphael.

"Will I see you again before I leave?"

"That's up to you, Eleni. You can still come with me. We can search for the source of the world. They say there's an island out there covered with strange trees and creatures that haven't been seen for thousands of years."

"Please, don't start that again."

"Then may your trip to Athens be full of adventure."

"I don't want any more adventure."

"Then happiness. May Allah grant us both happiness."

"We'll always be friends, Raphael."

"Life's not like that," he told her. "It's all meetings and partings. But I'll always come if I know you want me to."

"Will you?"

"Always, if I'm alive."

"I'll write you a letter," she promised.

"But you'll be back soon."

"Yes, of course," she said, but for the first time it occurred to her that she might not come back at all.

"Well then, onward, Christian soldiers. . . . I miss you already, Eleni. Maybe if I take a long swim I won't miss you so much." He started toward the water.

"Goodbye," she called after him, not loud enough for him to hear."Go with the good." Then she left him alone and carefree amid the waste of sand and phosphorescent water and the wash of shells and the things that live in the sea.

Eleni walked rapidly. She did not avoid the Turkish quarter, but this time the street was empty. At home, the old pistol-spring lock screamed under her key, but if her father heard, he made no sound. She went to her room, and she wanted to sleep so badly that she could not sleep at all. Ahead lay danger and unhappiness and sacrifice. It should make her proud. She was acting for Cyprus, for the boy she loved, for her mother. Then behind her closed lids she saw her mother, and her mother held a handkerchief to her mouth when she talked. Why did people have to be sick and helpless? Why did they have to gouge at one another?

She longed to ascend through the roof and fly away to another country where she would never again hear of these troubles. She would dwell in Athens forever. She would sell her paintings and be famous, and even as she told herself these things she knew they weren't true. She could never escape. She was not like Raphael; she did not believe in his mythical island. Even Raphael, was he as self-contained as he implied? Could he really sail away, she wondered. And where would he go? At least her dream was real and she would have it for a time. Athens! As she lay in bed waiting for sleep, she counted the days. She counted the days until Athens.

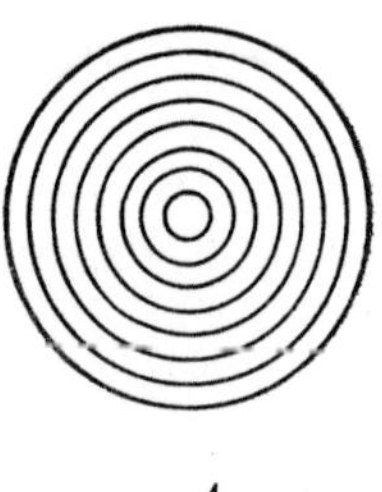

4

"I don't like it. I don't like your taking that message," he said.

"But there's nothing you can do about it," Eleni told him. She had baked the message into a loaf of bread for her mother. She was ready, and the bus would leave in a few minutes.

"It's my fault," said her father.

"Everything will be all right."

"It's my fault for letting you get into this," he insisted miserably.

The awning out front kept the interior of the shop dark. She could not see her father's face distinctly, and she was glad of that.

"What does the message say?" he asked her.

"I don't know. I folded it up."

"You don't want to talk about it?"

"No," she said gently.

He was only a dark silhouette there in the corner. His cigarette glowed bright, then dim.

"You're serious about marrying Phaethon, aren't you, Eleni?"

"I suppose so."

"It's not right for a woman to be alone. People don't like to see a woman alone. But an engagement's a serious thing. A contract, and rings."

"I know, Father. It hasn't come to that."

"I like Phaethon. I do," he said. "I don't want you to misunderstand. It's simply that some people seem born to bring more trouble than the rest of us. They're like unconscious carriers of disease."

"You mean Phaethon?"

"I didn't say that. . . . If it weren't for EOKA, and these bombings. . . . There'll be a trial, and all sorts of trouble, trouble for everybody. Father Grikos will be after me again about drugs for EOKA."

"He humiliates you, Father."

"We've got to put up with a lot of things in this world, Eleni. For your mother's sake. She's uncomplaining as a tree. If it weren't for this trouble, I'd be friendly with the English. They're all right. Didn't we fight side by side? I'll not forget that retreat. Funny, I never minded marching. There's a kind of poetry to an army on the march . . . funny." He actually laughed, but the laugh deteriorated into a thick cough. He shook backwards and forwards in an attempt to control it. "Well, we won't be friendly for a while, not with the trial. It's almost time for the news."

"Turn on the radio, Father. I have to go now." Eleni's voice was low and soft.

"News," said her father. "There's nothing to be done about it." He prodded at the radio as one might at an animal to see if it were dead.

Eleni told him goodbye. She went out the door and closed it behind her. She could hear the radio voice. She could almost see her father, in his old uniform, hunched over the radio. Then she stepped from under the awning, her eyes squinting because of the glare.

Eleni waited with a couple of old women in black for the bus from Ktima. The whitewashed wall was beginning to be warm from the sun and she patted it with her hand in time to a tune in her head. Finally the bus came into sight. Like a broken-down caterpillar, it inched along, stopping and starting as people got on and off. Eleni had to stand near the front and she knew she would stand the whole way to Ayios Dhimitrianos. From there she would walk to the monastery.

The bus raised so much dust that the windows were closed. Inside it smelled of sweat, and some of the women held the cool cut ends of cucumbers to their foreheads to keep from fainting. Outside the landscape passed in a blur of browns and yellows. At Tsada came the first long stop. Windows were thrown open and a camel driver brought jaffa oranges and tried to sell them to the passengers. Eleni had no money so she did not look at the oranges. She watched the camels, old and bony as archpriests, lying in the shade of a wall with their great legs folded under them. One of the camels made a continuous groaning noise. Then the bus started up again and the windows were closed. At last they reached the first foothills, low and trembling in the relentless light. A special stop was made near the Neophytos Monastery, and a priest got out. He would have to cross a ravine to get to his destination, for the monastery had begun as a hermit's cave in the cliffside. From here the road went up long white switchbacks between little valleys where the grapes were being harvested. On the hilltops, windmills turned and turned like rotating crucifixes.

Ayios Dhimitrianos was the end of the line. From there on, the road was too rugged for the bus. Gratefully, Eleni disembarked. Five miles of walking remained, but it would be better than the bus.

The glazed blue sky was already fusing with heat. She felt the sun prickle the back of her hands and tasted the dust. In the vineyards women were harvesting. At the wine press, young men trod the grapes until the juice trickled in a purple flow from the spout into the great amphorae. One boy with protruding teeth whistled at her. "Hey, there!" he called, and her smile won her a bunch of grapes. She ate them as she went along the road, which twisted back and forth. Up and up it went to the heights of contemplation, to the abode of the monasteries and the saints.

Just ahead were the first forests, with cedars and Aleppo pines, older than any recorded documents, where the mouflon roamed in shady solitude.

Despite her apprehensions, it was good to be young and healthy and in motion. She ran a few steps and then she walked. She never noticed the two soldiers until they strode into the middle of the road. It was an English check-point, and there was no turning back, for they had seen her and were waiting. She walked toward them. She wanted to appear nonchalant, but a cold rush of terror carried down her legs to her feet.

"Sorry, miss. May I see your pass?"

He was a young soldier, no older than Raphael, with a shock of pale hair like a ruffled crest on his forehead and pale blue Irish eyes that seemed stuck in his face like raisins on a sugar cooky.

"You speak Greek very well," she told him, and he did, with waspish authority.

"The pass, miss."

She fumbled in her basket. "Will this take very long?"

"As long as it has to."

Eleni held out the pass. "It's to see my mother." The soldier began to scribble in a small notebook. He made an erasure, then took down her name. He asked other questions and she had to ask him to speak louder. She couldn't seem to hear over the beating of her heart.

"There's no need to be distressed, miss. It's just routine," but his smile never broke into laughter and he asked to examine her basket. "Orders, you know." He went through everything. Her heart stopped beating at all. Then she realized the search was not going to discover anything. It was simply routine. He did not break open the loaves of bread.

Finally he handed the basket back to her. "We don't like this any better than you do, miss. Take care."

Until she was out of sight, Eleni could scarcely keep her feet from flying. And as soon as the road took a turn she left it and plunged into the woods. Here in the cathedral quiet she felt safe. The foliage made it dark, too, like the inside of a church, but it was not gloomy. There was little undergrowth and the well-spaced, tall trees were like a park. She glided noiselessly over the needle-hushed floor through endless green tunnels toward the monastery of Chrysorroyiatissa. Here dryads and nymphs might be hiding. She looked for their flashing white feet in the splashes of sunlight and listened for their laughter. She hoped they would preserve her from an encounter with the terrorists. There must be many men here in the mountains, hiding from the British, like Phaethon. She thought of the leader Afzendiou who had been cornered in a forest cave by the English and had held them off until a shell struck one of his ammunition boxes and the entire cave exploded. That was heroism, she supposed, but she didn't want glory for Phaethon at such a price.

At four thousand feet above the sea the forest thinned, yielding to the terraced fields of the monastery. As Eleni climbed, dusty spirals became black-gowned laborers. They were all strangers and she kept on toward the fire station. Father Constantine was always there during the dry season. He had told her that the forest of Troodos was his great garden, where every plant took over a century to grow.

The station was an old stone tower with a circular wooden walk. Incongruously, it contained modern spotting equipment and a direct telephone connection with the central station at Stavros. Father Constantine was standing outside on the platform, a pair of field glasses hung around his neck.

He greeted Eleni with a massive smile. Red from laughter and full of good nature, he reminded her of an aging cherub with a perpetual mouthful of cake.

"Worried about fires, as usual?" she greeted him.

"This time of year, it's the devil's preserve," said Father Constantine. "With lightning, and no rain, and these EOKA people. But it's good to see you, Eleni. Your mother has been asking. Come along. She'll be overjoyed."

"What about the EOKA people?" she asked him as they descended from the tower.

"They set fires. Only last week a stand of cedars went up in flames. The finest trees in the world." He had often explained to her that the trees of Cyprus were descended from the cedars of Lebanon, that their ancestors had masted the ships of Solomon and Rameses. "I don't understand those people. They have lived too long away from humanity. One day God will pay them back, never fear," and he added Isaiah for confirmation. " 'Yea, the fire of thine enemies shall devour them.' But that's no concern of yours . . ." and they went the rest of the way in silence, stopping only once for Eleni to drink a cup of water. From its taste she knew it was snow water that had come off the roof. There had been very little precipitation of any kind since spring.

The tubercular ward was on the southern side of the monastery grounds. It had been constructed out of local timber, with British help. Eleni's heart beat too fast; the corridors were as silent as death.

"I'll leave you, Eleni. Your mother's there." Father Constantine indicated a door and then went off. His slippers were noisy in the silence and he carried his fat in a contented way, as if his body contained money and security.

Eleni adjusted her face to a smile and opened the door. Even in the heat of the day, the room struck her as cold and hard, like a tomb without a cross.

"Mother?" she said.

The figure seated beside the window did not stir. In a moment of panic, Eleni thought her mother was dead. Then she saw that she was breathing. She planted a small cool kiss upon her forehead.

"My dear, I beg your pardon. I must have been daydreaming." The voice was soft and cobwebby.

"Of good things, Mother?"

"Of old things. Give me your hands." Her mother's hands were cool and frail, and so was her smile, but it was still wise and tender. Then they separated to scrutinize one another.

"Where on earth did you get that green dress?"

"Don't you like it, Mother?"

"I don't know. It's very green, isn't it?"

"How are you, Mother? You look well," lied Eleni.

"I feel like a piece of furniture in a repair shop. But forget me." Her eyes were wet. "I thought you wouldn't have time to come this far. Sit down . . . it's so hot. Sit down."

"Mother, it's true, you do look better. You'll be home

soon." But her mother's appearance was always a shock, her face as though it had suffered shipwreck. Demeter's celebrated beauty had all been stripped away. But she had adjusted to many things in life and had overcome many more. There was still strength in her face and a certain grandeur. The girl felt proud of her mother, proud of the way she sat with her back straight as though riding a horse. It was hard for Eleni to remember sitting on her mother's lap, touching that once beautiful face with her fingers, but her mother had been the guiding hand of her childhood. There had never been punishment. Good conduct had simply meant pleasing Mother; misconduct, making her sad.

"How is your father?"

"Well . . . he sends his best," said Eleni. Actually he had sent no message. "Father Grikos is always after him for drugs."

"There's a fury in that priest. He makes little distinction between his own and God's enemies. Does your father give him the drugs?"

"He does what Father Grikos tells him."

"Your father has worked hard," said Demeter, her voice high and coming in little spurts of effort. "He will hold on to what we have until his fingers are broken."

"Perhaps only his fingernails," said Eleni.

"Eleni, be still. . . . You wouldn't say such things if you understood him. You have no idea how hard your father tries. . . ."

"Why do you defend him so, Mother?"

That was it. He either could not or would not defend himself. Perhaps the need for the medical certificate made his position indefensible. Even about this, Eleni wondered. Was the sanitarium really doing her mother good, or was Demeter simply tucked away here?

"Eleni, if you feed a man and wash his clothes and have

his children . . . and mind his house . . . well." The words were almost sung; they were a little beyond the power of Demeter's lungs, so that she had to gasp for air. "You must realize that I love him still."

"I'm sure you do, Mother. I love him, too. It's just . . . well."

Demeter closed her eyes and drew a deep breath. "No, not love perhaps, but I'm used to him. He's still part of my life."

For Eleni the conversation was hopeless. "Listen, please, Mother," she said. "I have things for you. Some books, and some fresh bread. One of the loaves is special. It has a message, a secret one." Briefly, she explained Phaethon's predicament and her part in delivering the message at the old chapel. The words did not come as she had expected, but in an apologetic rush.

"I'm glad you're going to Athens," said Demeter abruptly. She pulled herself up straighter, adding, "I don't want to interfere, Eleni, but . . ."

"Then don't, Mother."

"Kindly lower that voice, young lady. I'm not deaf and I want you to listen."

"I thought you'd feel sorry for Phaethon."

"I do, but that's not the point. I don't like your becoming involved in political activities."

"You're old, Mother. Phaethon and I are young." Eleni had only meant that their interests were different, but immediately she realized she had said the wrong thing.

"I won't be around much longer to bother you. Meanwhile, I'm going to tell you what I think of Phaethon. He is not very mature. He's like a little boy with a big knife. First he tries it on a blade of grass, then on a tabletop. In the end he breaks it on a stone. I can't regard him as a very good companion for you." Eleni was pacing restlessly up and down the room, her hands hugged under her armpits. "And I wish you'd stop that. Eleni, please sit down."

"He loves Cyprus, Mother."

"Love isn't a simple word, Eleni. It can be an excuse for the burning of cities, for generations of bloodshed."

"And I think I love him."

"I know that, Eleni, and it makes me wonder whether you're growing up or down. I'd even rather you fell in love with that fisherman, what's his name—Raphael? He may be irresponsible, but at least he seems to enjoy life."

Eleni gazed at the floor.

"Are you listening to me? I wish you'd learn from my mistakes. I've found out one thing too late; that life is nothing but the happiness you get out of it. I doubt that Phaethon knows that."

"After Enosis, things will be different."

"After Enosis! Eleni, we have only a little time allotted. Enosis may never come. Do you think the British will give up an island as important as Cyprus because of a few boys with homemade bombs? And what if Cyprus becomes part of Greece? Will that be better? Greece is a poor land. They need heavy taxes, and an army. . . . But it is a beautiful land. I'm glad you're going there."

Both were silent, Eleni with her thoughts, her mother as she tried to catch her breath. She stirred the air with a black fan. "I left the window open," Demeter said. "There was a nice fresh breeze a few moments ago. Where has it gone?"

"You're lucky to be up here, Mother. The dust is terrible back home."

"I envy you Athens." Demeter's voice was wistful. "Do you know, when I was your age I wrote poetry? I thought it was good, too, and I would leave it around hoping that someone would read it. Nobody ever did. When you're in Athens, don't keep your paintings to yourself. Without a public, you'll give it up. I hope you become famous, Eleni. I hope you never come back here." After a long pause she added, as if surprised by her own thoughts, "The strange thing is, I mean that. This isn't a good place for a young girl. I don't know when it will be. And marriage isn't always an answer."

For the first time Eleni's dream seemed shaped into words. Painting, Athens, a career! She did not want to relive her mother's life, or the lives of the black-toothed, black-shawled women of Paphos. She wanted something more, and the answer seemed to lie in those three words.

"Will you be staying here tonight?" asked Demeter.

"Father Constantine said it was all right. I'll go home in the morning."

"You'll be wanting to deliver that message, won't you?"

"I should," said Eleni. "I thought of doing it the first thing, but I wanted to see you."

"Do you know where the old chapel is?"

"Yes. Do you think a monk will pick it up? I mean, do you think any of the monks may be part of EOKA?"

"There are hundreds of monks flapping about here. It would be a little strange if so vast a monastery didn't house a few wicked brethren."

"I'll go now," said Eleni.

"But come back early. We'll have kebab and fatcha. They feed us very well here. Have you ever tasted Yemen coffee with a speck of ambergris? Come back soon." Demeter pressed her kerchief to her face before she kissed Eleni. The girl pretended not to see that she was going to cry.

Eleni left the room with a sense of relief. She took a deep breath of clean, fresh air. "Poor Mother," she said aloud, but it was only dimly that she perceived Demeter's terrible loneliness.

The old chapel stood at the edge of the woods. Its battered arches and buttresses, overgrown with vines and pierced by trees, lay like the petrified bones of some fallen Titan. Eleni entered through the main arch and went straight to the sanctuary which contained the altar stone. This room was intact still. Even the glass was unbroken, and so old that the light came through lavender as into an undersea cavern. She looked once about, listened, then slipped the folded paper under the stone.

Her job done, she wanted to get away. She wanted quite literally to wash her hands. Passing again through the main arch, she came across a monk. He seemed to be idling there and looked harmless enough: pink in the face, like a freshly cooked shrimp, and with oddly sprouting sandy hair that was shrimplike too. As she passed without speaking, he made the sign of the cross in the air. When she had gone a few steps, she looked back; he had vanished. So he was the one. And from his hands into another's? She imagined a man running, bent double, leaping and gliding into the darker, more mysterious depths of the forest, through deep green tunnels to a primitive throne where the Leader would receive him. She imagined the terrible human machinery that made up EOKA. Did it all begin and end with the Leader, or was this struggle of EOKA only part of a larger struggle rooted in the generations, in the centuries going back to the Trojan War, to Cain and Abel? Perhaps it began with God. However small, she felt herself a part of that struggle now.

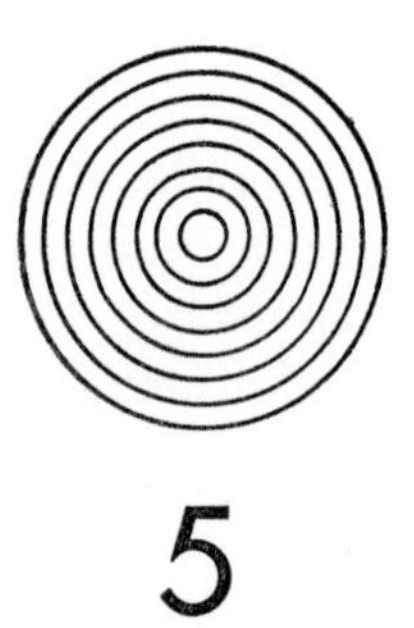

5

Eleni had never loved her room. Except for her paintings on the wall, it was sad and empty. She would not miss it. All her possessions had been packed into a single suitcase, her paints and brushes into a wooden box. The bed with its rope springs, the small bureau, and the incongruously large wall mirror would remain. "Goodbye, mirror," she said. She stared at the face reflected there. It was not an ugly face, but not one she found very interesting. She made a few expressions, was neither amused nor ennobled by her efforts, and went back to packing.

In the next room Father Grikos and Lazarus were talking; rather, the priest was sermonizing in a voice as loud as a church organ, and Lazarus was favoring him with murmurs of acquiescence.

"I'm here out of kindness," said the priest.

"Oh, I know it, I know it," came the reply.

As Eleni listened, Father Grikos explained how the British had intercepted so many of the munitions caiques that EOKA had devised another method of smuggling explosives. They would be placed inside china cats. It was up to patriotic merchants to subscribe.

"But explosives," protested Lazarus weakly. "Aren't drugs enough? I'd rather not be involved with explosives."

"Don't you think you're already rather deeply involved? After all, this is a time for sacrifice. My friend the village president isn't paid for his job. It's only out of good will that he issues medical certificates."

Whatever her father said in return, Eleni could not make out the words. His voice reached her as a slow droning monotone, without vitality. Angrily she forced her suitcase shut. "That's my father," she thought bitterly. "The head of this family. A man with any pride wouldn't sit there and be browbeaten." She pictured her father on the other side of the wall kneading his hands together and nodding to whatever the priest said.

"I was permitted to visit Stephan Diakos in the prison yard," Father Grikos said. "He is a brave boy. He's resigned to dying for his country. The British have no choice, of course. They'll have to hang him. That's the law. But they'll hang themselves along with him. It doesn't matter what he did. In every chapel and house all over Cyprus, men and women are praying for him. God will hearken to their prayers."

Eleni could not help listening. She seemed to see the room and her father grow smaller while the priest expanded, like a genii in the air.

"Presently Cyprus will have a martyr. After that, there will be no turning back. Cyprus will be Greek again." The priest's booming voice went on to picture an eventual war between Greece and Turkey, a war that would result in the re-establishment of the Holy Roman Empire, the recapture of Constantinople. Eleni was momentarily convinced by the fierce magic in the priest's words, then she rejected the whole idea. Stephan Diakos could never be a martyr. He was too ugly and mean, with wet slobbery teeth like a dog's. No holy war could come from such a martyr.

Eleni had to sit on the suitcase to get it to close. She drove the latches home with her fist. She was ready to leave, ready as she had never been for anything in her life. The Acropolis awaited her; the great statue of Athena swathed in ivory and gold; Pericles, the mighty statesman; Phidias, whom the ancient gods had set in heaven to sculpt the constellations.

All this was one day away, only one day. Meanwhile she would not listen to the priest's diatribe. She would not hang about in her room all day with nothing to do but make faces into the mirror. She had heard that Phaethon had gotten safely away, but suddenly she wanted to visit the tomb where he had hidden. She wanted to visit the beach where Raphael kept his boat, although he must be gone as well, with Jamal. In any event, she wanted to get out for a walk, a long one.

Eleni tried to pass through the room without acknowledging Father Grikos, but he called out to her. "You did a good thing for Phaethon. I'm proud of you."

How did he know? She looked at him, startled. The priest was obviously unaffected by her unreceptive manner.

"I've got good news for him," continued Father Grikos. "The child isn't going to die. She'll be all right, except for her hands."

"What do you mean, except for her hands?"

"They couldn't save her hands, my dear. Eleni, you must understand that God moves in mysterious ways, but whatever He does is right."

"Must God be brought into everything?" said Eleni. To be without hands seemed to her as bad as death . . . worse. She could imagine a dead child like a waxen doll set about with candles, but a child without hands—she closed her mind.

"Sometimes friendship makes me deaf," said the priest. "Every one of us must sacrifice something for Cyprus. Did you know the child, Eleni?"

"No. I want to go now. I'm in a hurry."

"Then I'm not sure I understand your concern. Is it Stephan? His life isn't wasted. Honestly, my dear, it will be a triumph."

"Why do you always say 'honestly,' and 'truthfully'? You always do, you know." She felt aggressive and ready to stand her ground.

Lazarus lifted his hands to adjust his necktie. Since it had been straight, the tug he gave it shifted it to one side. "Please, Eleni," was all he said.

"Yes, my dear," said the priest, "you should try to contain yourself. It doesn't become you. Eleni, I have to be honest with you. . . ."

"Every time you use that word you say something disagreeable," she told him. Her father half rose from his chair. He was in agony, and the knowledge only spurred her on. "If you want to manage my father's life, that's all right, but don't try to manage mine."

"Hear me, Eleni," said the priest, his voice tremulous with anger. With one hand he gripped his beard, and Eleni could imagine him tearing at it, furiously, and saying over and over, "Honestly, honestly, my dear."

"I won't put up with such impertinence," he said. "I will not have you running off to meet that excommunicant!"

"Raphael? So that's what you're thinking. Raphael's gone. You've frightened him away. You've frightened Father, too. Look at his mustache. See how big and patriotic it's getting?"

With this she departed, feeling she had left a dart behind her. Father Grikos turned, almost pirouetting on his umbrella, but he did not call out. He let her go.

Eleni burst through the door, stumbled on the cobblestones, but managed to keep her feet. "I hate them! I hate them! I hate them!" she told herself aloud, but when she turned the corner and stopped to catch her breath she began to cry. The sobs wrenched up agonizingly. She hated neither of them. For the moment she hated only herself. Why had she done that to her father? At the very least, she had always received from him a remote, impersonal benevolence. The failure was probably hers, rooted in the image she had once had of him, a soldier returning triumphant from the great war, whom time and her own growing up had turned into a small, cautious shopkeeper.

Eleni had half expected, half wanted to be followed. When no one came, she walked down the road. There a buzzard stood, like an old bald-headed man in a black shawl. It looked over its shoulder at her and then began its ungainly run and flight. Once clear of the ground, it soared.

She did not regret her conduct toward the priest except as it might affect Lazarus. Father Grikos could take care of himself. Always she had admired him as a painter, as a religious leader, and as a patriot, but in her feelings for him there was a new element, fear. Like a bottle of nitroglycerine, Father Grikos seemed a danger to himself and to anyone with whom he associated.

These problems concerned her until she reached the

beach. There was no sign of Raphael's boat. The waves had eradicated even the imprint of its hull upon the sand. She went out on the stone breakwater, where the old fishermen with their blue-white mustaches and leathery faces sat patching their nets. It seemed as tireless and infinite a task as the spinning of the fates. Here the lapping waves were as clear as holy water. She could see to the bottom, where the octopuses twined among the mossy stones and the fish kept themselves steady in the current with wavering fins. From the fish she could tell that the current was strong. It must be pulling at the bottom of Raphael's boat, and she wondered if he could feel its pull through the tiller.

Far out a tiny sail, like a scarlet blossom, rocked over the high sea. It came into her sight from time to time and then disappeared. She knew it was not Raphael's sail—his sail was gray. But she pretended it was his. Sitting on the breakwater, she let her eyes fix upon the empty horizon, waiting for dreams to come. What if she wrote him a note and left it at his shed? It wouldn't matter what she wrote, for she did not expect to see him again. "I miss you, Raphael." She could begin that way. What if she began, "I love you"? She did, in a way—not romantically, but as the person she felt closer to than anyone else. So she would begin that way, "I love you"—and then what? And what would be his answer? She could not imagine. "I want you to come back to Cyprus, Eleni." That didn't sound like Raphael, and so she gave it up. She could not imitate him. Instead, she said a prayer, "May your tiller always rest lightly in your hands, and under your eyes may the sea be calm and the sky blue." That was pretty, she thought, and it made her feel sad.

If she never came back from Athens, she would not see Phaethon again either. That was a shock, like breaking an engagement. He might be a great man one day, and he was handsome, and lovable as a little boy when he was afraid. His hands were fine and supple. Raphael's hands were like a great turtle's, hard, almost scaly from the sea. He probably had fish scales all over, but his laugh always made her want to laugh.

Yes, she thought, when it came to goodness, Raphael was the better man of the two. He was more than a man, he was like a breeze from far-off places. She could feel that breeze stirring now in her bones. But it was an actual breeze that fretted the water and blew hair into her eyes, the September wind from Turkey which brought the migrant vultures. In hundreds they circled high on the thermals, tilting only enough to catch the gusts like the sails of a ship. Thousands of feet over Cyprus they flew, then swept off on their winter journey to Africa. Well, tomorrow she too would bathe in the sky, only higher and faster. She felt young and ready, at the beginning of life, and all of it lay ahead.

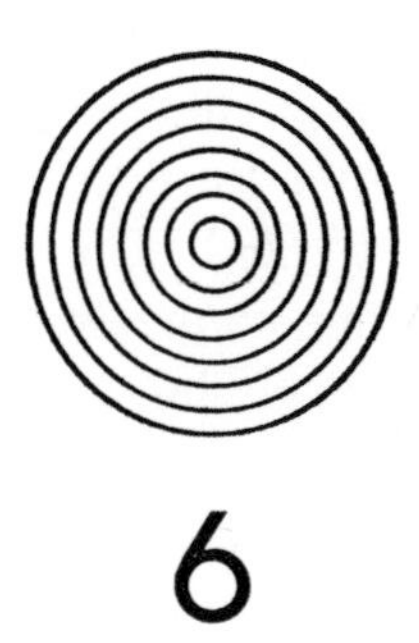

6

There was the feel and the smell of dawn long before the light. Eleni rose in darkness and dressed slowly. There was no need to hurry. The night was over and she would never go back to where she had been before she put on her clothes. She walked from room to room in the silent house. Excited and afraid, she hugged to herself the knowledge of her imminent departure.

When the sun shone red through the windows, she went to the chapel to apologize to Father Grikos and to ask his blessing. She feared the meeting and hoped the priest would not be there, but he greeted her at the door and seemed all benevolence.

Immediately he brushed aside her apologies. "So today

you take to the air. You know, I've never flown. I don't think I ever shall until I sprout wings and assume the form of an angel." Together they went inside the chapel to pray. They knelt side by side, and Father Grikos patted his hands softly together as he prayed aloud. Eleni tried to listen to him, but her eyes kept wandering to the frescoed saints and she idly wondered how all their eyes had come to be scratched out.

"We now commit this dear child to Thy loving care. Watch over her. She is our hope. Amen," concluded Father Grikos. Eleni crossed herself, took incense and oil, and went up to light the lamp of the Madonna.

Outside again, she made an effort to praise the priest's painting. He said, "God built a whole world in a week and had time to rest. I've only added a few figures to this little world," and he pointed them out, all warriors, some still fighting, some stretched on the ground, and one being led away in chains.

The bus for Nicosia left at seven. Eleni had expected to go alone and was both touched and chagrined when her father appeared in his best suit of heavy wool and his stiff Sunday shoes. He went first with the suitcase and found a seat and saved one for her. As usual, the bus was late in starting. There was a dispute because a farmer wanted to take two pigs aboard without paying their fare. "They aren't people, are they?" But by 7:15 every seat was taken and folding stools filled the aisle. The people waited expectantly, and Eleni could tell from their faces that they were proud to travel by motorbus. Finally, the door was slammed, the bus shivered like a mastodon dreaming in its sleep, and they were off, the hood cracking and flapping.

They passed the roadway shrine on the Limassol road. Its oil lamp still glowed red. Eleni threw one backward glance at the old walls of the port, at the Turkish privies with their sea-blue domes, and then dust obscured it all.

At Kouklia, where Aphrodite's temple once stood, women

sorted a field of coppery onions. There was a roadblock, and the English conducted a laborious search, even poking through the oilskin schoolbags of the children. Then the bus roared on toward Limassol. "I'll be getting off here on the way back," said Lazarus. These were the first words he had spoken and they brought disappointment to Eleni. She should have realized he would not go so far simply to keep her company. He would be placing an order for china cats in Limassol.

The bus stopped in Limassol for half an hour and was searched again. The children left and some monks got on. The door clanged and they were off, passing Amathus, where Richard the Lion-Hearted had been married eight hundred years before. Neither Eleni nor her father had spoken again.

The longest part of the trip was from Limassol to Nicosia. Here the mountains gave way to a flat autumn landscape of yellowish purple spotted like a leopard skin with small shrubs. In this almost featureless plain, the bus rushed by a great wire enclosure full of men, an unintelligible blank multitude.

"What's that?" exclaimed Eleni in surprise.

"It's a prison—for EOKA. The English put them there when they can catch them."

She watched the blur of wire and faces, a thousand eyes, a thousand shoes, all alike in the dust. The camp passed, only barren hills remained when she became aware that her father was speaking in a low, strained voice. "Eleni, I'd like to talk to you, and I don't know quite what to say." She stiffened, still looking out of the window. "Eleni, I know that you hate me."

"Hate you!" she echoed, appalled that he should think such a thing. "Father, I don't!" She seemed to see him with telescopic clarity, an aging man, eyes with the dreams burnt out of them, hair heavily greased and absurdly parted down the middle. That was her father, and he was asking for help she could not give.

"I'm not angry, Eleni, about yesterday. I don't mind what you said. It's probably true." He looked at her so forlornly that she wished he would strike her instead. "Things aren't the way I would have them. I've made a lot of mistakes, but I want you to believe this. What I've done, I've done for you and your mother . . . haven't I? Eleni, I've never lied to you."

"Nor have I to you, Father."

"I'm glad we can be honest with one another."

Honest about what? Had they ever really communicated? She felt as though a rope were twisted tight inside her body, and it was beginning to kink.

The driver was waging a ceaseless battle with the road. Another search took place at Laxia, and then they entered the suburbs of Nicosia. The bus stopped. The passengers streamed away. Her father hailed an ancient saloon taxi with flowered curtains at the windows. Through a great hole in the floor, Eleni watched the road pass. She wanted to tell her father that everything was all right, that she loved him, that the world was beautiful. The words didn't come. Finally he spoke, but it was of practical things.

"You've got your passport?"

"Yes." She touched it.

"And money?"

She felt for her purse.

"Eleni, you must give my best regards to my brother. I haven't seen him in years, you know, but we were great friends."

"He was a hero, wasn't he?"

Lazarus had always made much of his brother, and for Eleni he had become the intrepid image her father once had been.

"Yes, a great hero. They gave him a job with the government because of his wound. He must have a very grand house."

"And servants?"

"He has never written of servants. It's good of him to let you live with them."

Yes, it was very good of him. Second only to standing upon the Acropolis, she looked forward to meeting her uncle.

The taxi had emerged from the suburbs. In the distance Eleni saw airplanes at rest. She felt suddenly cold. Her father paid the cab and took her bag to the BEA loading desk. Most of the passengers seemed to be British, some of them children returning to England for the autumn school term.

Eleni waited in line at customs. Once she passed through, they would be separated. For a moment, her father placed his hand on hers.

"Father?"

"I guess I never counted on one thing," he said.

"What's that?"

"Your growing up."

They stared silently at each other for a long, revealing moment. She sensed that he understood her dream of escape, her intention not to return. She tried to think of something to say, something to bridge so many years of not really communicating. It was with relief that she heard herself being called by the customs man to present her passport. She gave her father a kiss on the cheek.

"Eleni . . ."

The loudspeaker broke in. The schoolchildren pushed toward the boarding gate. She hesitated, but the moment had passed. She followed the crowd and her father went in the other direction, shaking his head.

•

Eleni had strapped herself in on the instructions of the stewardess. As she waited in the great machine of glass and aluminum, she was sure of only one thing. It would never take off.

Beyond the glass, across a strip of asphalt, a tiny black figure stood still as a statue, arms resting on the top of a picket fence. For an unaccountable moment she wanted to run and bury her face in his woolly jacket. It wasn't too late, and her hands were actually fumbling with the latch of her safety belt when a small boy's voice spoke.

"I say, is this seat taken?" He wore blue shorts and a blue lettered cap, and he was very English-looking. "You are Turkish, aren't you?" She had had enough English in school to tell him she was Greek. "Then I don't suppose you'd want me to sit down," he said, but he didn't retreat.

"Sit down. Don't be silly." She patted the seat.

"Thanks awfully."

By this time the plane's door was sealed. Her father still stood by the fence. From a duct above her head, music had begun to play. It seemed a foreign sort of music and it made her feel the world was large and strange.

"Good afternoon," said the loudspeaker. "This is Captain Gamage, welcoming you to flight . . ." With a shudder the engine sneezed out some pale blue smoke. The metal, fabric, and glass of the huge machine began to shudder as the plane turned slowly. The tiny figure was gone from sight.

Sunlight gushed into her eyes as they turned in a circle, then rolled slowly away. Eleni gripped the arms of her seat. She must have looked alarmed, for the boy said, "Not yet. I do this lots. They have to rev her up first." She didn't understand. The boy tried a few Greek phrases; he gesticulated. Their communication became a game of charades, and it helped Eleni relax until the plane began to shake as though it had just received an unexpected injection of fuel. It will sit here and shake itself to pieces, she thought, but it began to move. It became a bright, roaring, hurtling cave, while from the ceiling duct poured soothing music.

"Don't worry. It'll be all right," said the boy. "Say, we're doing all right . . . talking. Your English isn't a bit bad, honestly. Is this your first time in an airplane? It's not half so dangerous as autos, really."

The buildings of Nicosia seemed to be rushing toward them. Pilgrims from Jerusalem began singing a hymn, and Eleni knew this was the moment of her death. The vibrations lessened, then ceased altogether, as the whole flat expanse of Cyprus withdrew. They were in the air and it wasn't death any more. At the age of seventeen she felt she was witnessing her own birth.

"You see?" the boy told her, grinning.

The pilgrims no longer sang. There was a general relaxing and rustling of magazines. Eleni's ears began to accustom themselves to the drone and whistle of the engines.

"Look, you can see the Taurus Mountains in Turkey over there. In spring, when I come back, they'll have snow." The boy sounded sad. "Are you off on a long trip, too?"

"Yes, very long."

Soon they were over the Troodos mountain range. The peaks pushed up through pine forests. Winter snows had polished them slippery-black and glinting, and it seemed to Eleni that if all the mountains of the world were old, certainly those of Cyprus were the oldest.

"That's where we used to go summers," said the boy.

"Your father's with the government?"

"Oh, yes. Last summer we stayed in Nicosia and went to Kyrenia on weekends. We didn't dare stay in the mountains. They say it's simply packed with Cyp guerrillas. . . . Are you EOKA?" he asked hopefully.

"Would you like me to be?"

"Actually, if you were the Leader with a ten thousand pound reward, I would."

Eleni smiled. She wondered if there was a reward for Phaethon. He must be down there in the secret glens of the Troodos. From above, the forests did not seem large enough to conceal so many men.

Gradually mountains gave way to plains and then the long white line of the coast. The sea seemed very deep and she could see down into it. She could see the winged arrow of the plane on the water, and wondered if it frightened the fish. There was a caique below and she thought of Raphael. It was too big for his *Nereid,* but he must be there somewhere, perhaps watching the plane and thinking of her.

"I bet it's full of explosives," said the boy.

"No, china cats," she told him.

"You're a funny one. I like you."

Astern, the land was sinking low and dying away. Ahead was the unending expanse of the sea.

"They do get bombs, though," he said. "A few weeks ago they just missed Government House. It woke me up. They dropped a whopping great bomb on our house, too."

"Was anyone hurt?"

"Well, actually it isn't a house. It's a foundation. My dad's building a house out at Kyrenia." The boy explained how hard it had been to get building materials to Kyrenia. Then as soon as the materials were together, all the workmen had gone off to harvest. He sounded very serious, like an old man. Then suddenly he became a boy again. "Look! There's Crete. We had a wizard time in Crete!"

For Eleni, the past and the future seemed to float beneath her. There was a change now in the sea. It looked blacker and feathered with whitecaps. She thought of Theseus and Jason, wondered why Homer had called it the wine-dark sea.

"You know why I didn't think you'd like me to sit by

you?" the boy asked. "It's that mess in Paphos. Dad says when we hang that bomber fellow all the Greeks will hate us. Do you believe he really threw the bomb and killed those chaps?"

"Yes," said Eleni.

"Oh. Why do you think so?"

"Because I know him."

"Wizard! You actually know him? He wouldn't be your steady? . . . Wait till I write home and tell how I met a friend of that bomber fellow!"

Eleni made no denials. It was hard now to remember what an unpleasant person Stephan had been. "He's a great hero in Paphos," she said.

Here the loudspeaker interrupted. Thunder squalls and turbulence were expected on the approach to Athens. The passengers were advised to fasten their seat belts. Already the sea was beginning to vanish under a crisscrossing of long cloud streamers which gradually thickened and became solid.

Glasses and bottles rattled noisily in the pantry. A light panel fell from the ceiling with a crash. Without warning, the plane seemed abruptly to lift, and then it dropped about three hundred feet. Luggage rattled down, a stewardess sprawled in the aisle. Someone screamed and Eleni found herself being hugged tight by her companion. As far as his seat belt would permit, the English boy had flung himself into her lap. His head pressed so hard into her throat that she could hardly breathe.

"It's all right," she said soothingly. "We're steady now."

Shamefacedly, he relaxed his hold. "You must think I'm a frightful coward."

"I was frightened, too," she told him.

The pilgrims were again singing a hymn, and the recorded music had begun to play once more.

Presently a long brown coastline came into view, and a

city with a graceful curve of mountains behind it. Where the sun dropped a solitary beam, the Acropolis rose like a golden toy. Eleni wanted to shout aloud, for it was a call of life to her soul. Even if she died right now in this plane, she would die knowing that she had reached Athens, that her dream hadn't been just a dream after all.

Individual buildings became distinct, a beach where people were swimming, and then the gray expanse of the airport. Their shadow rose as if to strike the ship. A hedge flashed by, and with a screech they struck the runway. Eleni was thrown forward against her seat belt. The propellers flickered and slowed, and the plane stopped completely before a silvery hangar.

With her disembarkation card clutched tight in her fist, Eleni prepared to leave the plane.

"I'll be staying on," said the boy. "I'm going to London, you know."

"I hope you have a good flight."

"Sometimes when it's foggy we have to go on to Prestwick, or Shannon, even." He was poised, a world traveler again. "I wish you were coming all the way."

"That would be fun," she said.

She stood in the aisle waiting for the other passengers to leave.

"One day I'll show you London," he said.

"I'll look forward to that."

The file of passengers began to move. The stewardess said goodbye and Eleni followed the others to the customs house. Looking back once, she saw a blue cap at the plane window; a hand waved. She waved back. She didn't know his name, would never know it. He must be headed for one of those schools in green English countryside where well-regulated little boys kicked viciously at soccer balls and learned about the Empire. He seemed to be a nice boy. She hoped that school, wherever it was, would not change him.

The airport was much the same as the one in Cyprus. There was the same snarl of voices, the same confusion, only here the loudspeaker babbled first in Greek, then in English. Eleni knew she would not be met at the airport. She was to take the bus to Constitution Square in the city, and there her aunt would be waiting for her. The bus was not as old as the one in Cyprus, and not as crowded. It rattled along the coast past small cafés and lidos. But it was the city Eleni had longed to see, and her first impression was disappointing. Athens was as big as she had expected, but it was ugly and new, block after block of apartment houses and offices, many of them unfinished, towering skeletal affairs seemingly more abandoned than the occasional vestiges of ancient times. She craned about to locate the Acropolis once again, but the new buildings were too tall.

In Constitution Square the passengers were disgorged, baggage was claimed, and the smell of exhaust was exchanged for that of dusty cement and roasting coffee beans. Everywhere she looked, there were signs of demolition and creation: mounds of sand, concrete mixers, wheelbarrows piled with shovels. They seemed to be tearing up good streets. The noise was so loud no one would hear her if she called for help. The hooting of trucks, the chatter of steam drills assailed her ears. Could anyone paint, let alone think, in such a place? For the first time Eleni experienced the depression of uprootedness.

If only Aunt Vasso or Uncle Andreas had met the bus. She looked wildly about for them, then remembered she had never met either one. She felt for an address in her purse. She showed it to a street peddler, an ancient man with sponges girded about him who looked like a barnacled crab. He couldn't read and he wasn't interested; he tried to sell her a sponge.

"Prizes! Prizes!" shouted a lottery salesman. His lottery slips were attached to a white bamboo cane, and from the way he tapped the ground Eleni knew he was blind. She was about to appeal to a tourist policeman with large white cuffs when she heard her name spoken aloud. She turned.

"Are you Eleni from Cyprus? You paint?"

The question came from a small woman in an ankle-length black skirt. The impression was wholly of blackness: black shoes, black hair tied with a black ribbon and covered with a black scarf. Only the face seemed gray, like scoured pumice stone.

"Aunt Vasso!" exclaimed Eleni with relief. She embraced her aunt, but the greeting was not returned. Her aunt simply moved her mouth, an expression that Eleni in time would recognize as a smile, even as she would come to know that her aunt dyed everything about her black: all her own clothes, all her husband's shirts, even the napkins on the table.

"Come with me," said Vasso.

Eleni hefted her luggage. "Have you a car?"

Her aunt looked at her, her eyes as expressionless as burnt holes in a towel. "It isn't far," she said.

"I can pay for a cab."

"Don't waste your money. It's not far," replied her aunt, making no move to assist even by carrying the paint box. "Is your scholarship very generous? Your father didn't mention that."

"Just a small living allowance and tuition."

"You'll be turning some of that over to my husband for food?" said the woman in a singsong, high-pitched voice which had begun to remind Eleni of needles and pins.

"Oh yes." The subject of board money had been mentioned in their correspondence. "My father talks so much about your husband. I'm sorry he didn't come. Will he be at home?"

"Oh, he'll be there."

Eleni was disappointed that her uncle had not come to

meet her. On very little evidence, it was true, she had come to idealize him into the sort of man she would have liked her father to be.

"Has he a government job?"

"Yes, on the Acropolis. He was a war hero, you know, and they gave him a government job after the Communists were defeated."

The streets were beginning to narrow, the buildings to shrink. Here shop boys stood on guard over barrels of pigs' cheeks, and blue smoke belched from tiny bakeries where ring loaves and spinach pastries were piled high.

"They call this the Flea Market," said Vasso. "We live in the Plaka. It isn't far." But the street was steep and the crowd jostling. Above all, Eleni was aghast at the signs of crushing poverty.

"My family came here in the 1920's. We were refugees from Turkey like your father. All the people in the Plaka once came from Turkey." The small, closely packed buildings looked like a band of refugees, huddling together against assault. She would practically have to break her neck to see the stars in this place.

"Is it much farther?" asked Eleni.

"Beyond that tavern and around a corner," said the woman, who hurried along with head bowed, oblivious as a burrowing mole.

The taverna was called the "Drunken Boat." Already several old gentlemen sat outside at small white tables sipping water. From within came the discordant sounds of a bouzouki being tuned.

Aunt Vasso scuttled around the corner. Here was the last street of houses; above was a precipitous slope planted with a few tall cypresses. She indicated a doorway, saying, "We have to live near the Acropolis because of my husband's job, you know."

Eleni set her bags down in the street. She had been too

tired to realize that above her towered the Acropolis. With the knowledge, her weariness seemed swept away.

"Come along," said her aunt. "You'll want to get settled. You'll want to meet my husband."

The doorway was somehow sinister: low, black, and crooked. It almost seemed to squint. Strangest of all, instead of steps there was a ramp of stone, heavily grooved. Eleni walked up the ramp and entered the front room. There it was night. The windows were shuttered and the narrow street let little light through the door. She felt as though she were in a large coffin.

"Here is my husband," said Aunt Vasso, with the air of someone handing over a parcel.

With a barrel-like trunk and a bull neck, his shoulders heavily cased in muscle, he loomed in the poor light like a boulder.

"Well, well, well! So this is Eleni. Introductions entirely unnecessary. I've heard a great deal about my talented niece." His voice was deep and rough, as masculine as an unshaven chin. "Come here, Eleni. Let me see you."

She went to him, her feet like lead anchors. "Don't be shy. I can't very well pounce on you." His slow smile spoke of good fellowship and spontaneity, but to Eleni a grim past screamed through that smile.

He looked at her very sternly, then solemnly winked. "We'll get on," he said.

"Have you a government job on the Acropolis?" she asked, suddenly disbelieving.

His whole great body shook with laughter until finally he subsided, rubbing his knuckles into his eyes. "Is that what the woman of the house told you? A government job? . . . Eleni, I sell postcards. That's all I'm good for."

For an instant Vasso's eyes flared, then the light went out of them again. "I've done it again. Look at my poor wife's face. If her eyes were pistols, I'd be a dead man."

Eleni stood horrified, confused.

"I'm sorry, Eleni. You're tired. You'll want to see your room. It's not much. I wish we didn't have to ask you to pay for it, but that can't be helped."

"He means we're poor," interjected Vasso.

"My capital isn't of this world," intoned the man.

"Come along," said the woman, and Eleni followed her up the stairs. Each step had a different voice, and the air smelled of mold and rodents. Her room was small with a high ceiling. Whitewash and cobwebs seemed all that kept it from collapsing with a rumble into the alley below.

"I'd have tidied up," said Vasso, "but with outside work . . ."

"I'll manage," said Eleni, weakly. "Just let me rest for a while."

Eleni was left alone. She sat on the edge of an unmade German army cot. The only other piece of furniture was a bureau fashioned of old wooden cartons wired together. The one small slash of a window looked out upon Lycabettus with its yellowish limestone peak and white chapel, but the sight gave her no joy. She wanted to blot it all out, to go home. She shut her eyes and told herself it wasn't real, but the bouzouki kept scratching, scratching from the nearby tavern. "He doesn't exist. That can't be my uncle. He isn't completely there." She felt weak and sick, remembering him propped on a cart with the stumps of his legs bound up in his trousers like poorly wrapped packages of meat.

"Mother of God, help me," she said. She kept her eyes closed, while below in the alley a beggar's voice rose, mocking, haunting. "In the name of pity, in the name of pity . . ."

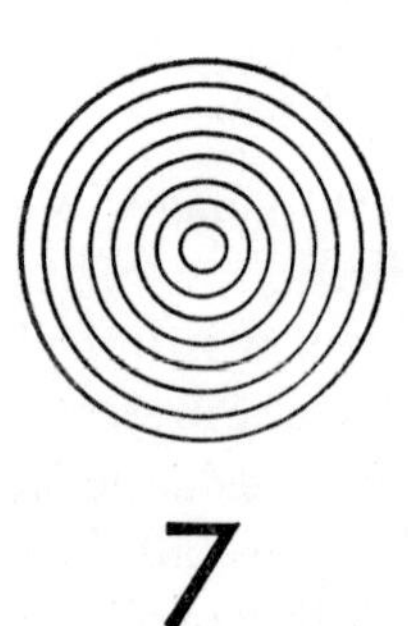

7

The following day Eleni registered at the university. The demands of her scholarship turned out to be very light; frighteningly so. Classes were optional. She had merely to paint and once a week report to an assigned professor for criticism and guidance. He was a tottery old fellow with a sad white mustache and tremulous hands. She knew at once that he had no technical skill to offer her. But he possessed a strong sense of history, and she went to him faithfully to learn about the city and how it had changed.

He advised her where to paint. Not the Acropolis at first; that was too much of a challenge to begin with. So she set up her canvas outside the old marble university buildings where students gathered to discuss Kazantzakis and the poems of Cavafy. And they flirted and made jokes in the king's Greek, which she could not understand. Then her professor recommended Lycabettus, which offered a view of the entire city, and dutifully Eleni trudged up the steep hill to sit panting at the top, where an old woman sold peppermint water from a pushcart. Sometimes, if Eleni was early, they ascended together, and it was Eleni who had to pause, though the cart on its three bicycle wheels looked like a match for a stevedore. "Practice, it takes a lifetime of practice," explained the vendor, and hiking up her skirt and sundry petticoats, she would proudly display a horrifying pair of legs: knotted and corded with muscles which a blue translucent skin scarcely managed to contain.

Recovering herself, Eleni would paint the dark interior of the Chapel of Saint George, where his icon stood with raised spear perpetually on guard. Must her right hand become enlarged, muscled like the old woman's legs before she was pleased by a day's work? Would it take even longer? She painted the Acropolis in the smoky distance and was not satisfied. "I wish you'd leave the Acropolis alone," complained her professor. "So many young people come to Athens thinking only about that place. It isn't Athens at all, Miss Lambros. For you with your narrow background, it's a skeleton. Paint flesh, Miss Lambros. Paint life. If you paint nothing but the Acropolis, you'd end up sketching for an archaeologist." He suggested she take the subway to Piraeus, which he described as a colorful kaleidoscope of ships and shops and people of all nations.

Eleni acknowledged his advice, but only after making herself a silent promise. For a few stolen hours, she would bathe in the light of the Acropolis. She chose the very next day and arrived at dawn. With the rising light it seemed that she had indeed found the dazzling center of the universe that swept away all residue of dark from her eyes. For her easel she chose a small terrace where a lookout had been built a hundred years before. When Germany had taken Athens in 1941, a Greek sentinel had been ordered to haul down his country's flag, and with the banner wrapped about his body he had flung himself from this spot. Here a poet had committed suicide because he had no hope of challenging such beauty. Eleni felt giddy in these surroundings. She could almost see the poet with the muzzle pressed against his temple waiting for the sun to rise, the sentinel poised for an instant in the air like a bird in flight. She could sense their feverish joy. Nevertheless, she placed her canvas well away from the brink.

No scrambling tourists intruded upon her efforts, though by midmorning they arrived in crowds. She was Phidias gazing at a new creation, and those who surrounded her were tunicked philosophers and statesmen: Thucydides speaking of military affairs in Sparta; Protagoras arguing with Prodicus and Hippias; Pericles declaring, "For we are lovers of the beautiful, yet simple in our taste." Throughout the morning she was filled with these imaginings and regarded herself purely as the medium of their transmission. She meant to stay all day and watch the white lights of Athens brighten the parks and buildings like a thousand candelabra, but her euphoria began to fade. By midafternoon she was aware of the tourists stumbling over loose stones, taking pictures, commenting on her efforts in foreign tongues. More disturbing still was Andreas. Clean and legless, he sat on his small cart amid the crowd moving about beneath the temple of Athena Nike. Too far away for conversation, he still managed an occasional grin and cheerful wave which she could not ignore, until his ruined presence seemed to blanket the entire Acropolis. With these distractions came hunger and a nasty suspicion that by early evening was an absolute conviction. Her picture was trash. Except for the cost of canvas, Eleni would have torn it to shreds. "Why does he have to be here?" she muttered to herself. "Why do they all have to come stumbling around?" She scraped a day's paint back onto her palette.

She made no attempt to start over. But for Andreas, she would have gone home immediately. She thought at first she might avoid him by lingering late, but when dusk came he was still there. Slowly she put away her paints and the Acropolis seemed suddenly too dark, too empty, too full of night and the oncoming winter. Then she went to Andreas and smiled and walked home by his side, the whole tortuous way. His shoulders had trained themselves high from the strain of propelling the cart by hand, and through his shirt they showed the massive strength of an uprooted tree.

Next morning she walked to Omonia Square and took the subway. At the Theseion Station it emerged into dusty sunlight and a few minutes later arrived at Piraeus, the end of the line. Where the walls of Themistocles once stood, she found breweries, macaroni factories, and tall black chimneys belching forth the acrid residue of chemical manure. The hurly-burly of Piraeus took her and bore her about as the ocean does driftwood, down streets of shabby awnings where fly-blown oranges and tomatoes lay on brilliant papers, tempting with color in spite of the flies. Like stalactited caves were the shops of artisans, where knives and scissors and shoes hung down in bunches from the ceilings. Caverns too were the wholesale wine shops. Lit by naked light bulbs, casks climbed one another to the ceilings, and clerks and customers had to watch their step for the bottles scattered across the floors. What a city it was! Instead of being uplifted, Eleni was stupefied. Even with her eyes closed, her ears covered, she could not escape. Its aromatic essence would live on in her nostrils: fresh bread, roasting coffee beans, rotting oranges, rancid oil, new wine, belched garlic, the exhaust fumes of a bus. Overwhelmed by it all, Eleni never once unlimbered her canvas.

For composure she sought the sea. The great harbor with its forest of masts and rigging derricks seethed with shipping from Egypt, Turkey, Israel, Great Britain, Germany. Here the smells were of fish and tar and briny nets. Eleni stared in amazement at the rusty hulks of Libery ships, at massive bales of merchandise, at the water where bits of cork bobbed in yellow scum and rainbow pools of oil. A small, rust-streaked steamer called *Despina* was embarking with a merry crowd for the pleasure islands of the Aegean. A ferryboat from Salamis arrived with a cargo of seasick nuns sniffing lemons under their shawls. This was no place to set up her canvas. She continued to wander up and down as if she really knew what she was looking for.

Eleni found her place at last in the Tourkolimano, a little crescent-shaped harbor of open cafés. Fishing caiques and small yachts were anchored there, and at the cafés old men sat around little tables with their bubbling narghiles and made up lies about their neighbors. Here fishermen slept all day on their rocking boats with only a strip of canvas between themselves and the sun. She had to stop somewhere, and this had at least the pace and flavor of Paphos.

At the western end, near the Hellenic theater, she set up her canvas. There, amid the windy sunlight of space and September, she began really to paint: cerulean blue for the sky, cobalt for the water, with a touch of burnt sienna and black where it mirrored back the masts. How lovely the paint was, freshly spread on the canvas, glistening, full of life. She could have licked it off with her tongue. She worked steadily. No one paid her the slightest attention until she stopped in midafternoon for lunch. At one of the waterside cafés she ordered bread and sardines and a glass of Fix orangeade. She might not have noticed the waiter at all if he hadn't said, "Well, miss, so you think you're an artist."

Eleni smiled up at him. "Actually, I'm only . . ." It was the necktie that stopped her. Rare as it was for a café waiter to wear a tie at all, this one was brilliant red and had embroidered on it a naked dancer.

"A student?" he added. "I thought so. On a scholarship? You're not from around here, that's plain enough. You probably won't believe this, miss, but I had a scholarship. Yes, I really did. Music. I went to the States and ended up in a Coney Island hash house, and all I got for it was this necktie and a nickname. Around here they call me Brooklie. For Brooklyn, you know?"

There wasn't much more to their conversation. Eleni went back to her painting, and when she left for home the waiter waved goodbye. That made her feel good and she knew she would return to Tourkolimano the next day. She knew, too, that she had made a good start. The basic lines of her painting as she studied it that night stood up strong and clean.

Eleni returned to the small harbor the following day and every day after that. Except for her mealtime exchange with Brooklie, she was alone, but she felt at home, and she felt she was doing good work. Her professor agreed with her. The early autumn days passed into a routine that seldom varied. Then in the middle of October an alien ship appeared in the little harbor. She noticed it first at the harbor mouth, caught like an old rocking horse in the waves that broke over the small wheelhouse. Though Eleni was no expert on boats, she knew it was from Cyprus even before it panted up to its mooring. With a cough the motor died. A woman with the black hooped hood of a Maltese scurried to the bow and dragged a weedy float from the water. Slowly the boat swung around in the wind, and Eleni read the writing on the stern. "Limassol, Cyprus." Presently a skiff put off from the stern. The woman sat in the bow while a man rowed them ashore. Without waiting to secure the skiff, the woman scuttled away. As Eleni watched, the man looped a line around a bulkhead and then he, too, went ashore. He walked strangely, with one hand held out in front like the paw of an animal, as though he moved through a fog. She observed as he passed that his face was a sailor's face, flinty from weather and salt, with the cold bleak eyes of one who is familiar with wintry seas. Having passed, he stopped and turned around to stare at her, until she had to duck her head and pretend she had been painting all along. When she looked up, he was gone.

Like the passage of so many strangers, Eleni forgot about the sailor until late in the afternoon when she heard the clap of sandals moving toward her. She looked up.

"You!" he said. There was no other person nearby whom he might be addressing. "You're Eleni?"

"How do you know my name?" she said, and stood up.

"Don't run away scared," said the sailor, catching hold of her arm. "Listen, I'm a friend of a friend, so to speak." But he didn't let go, and his grip was firm. Though she was taller than he, she did not think of him as a small man, for his trunk was thick and his arm heavy and sinewy as a smithy's. The black hairs that covered it were beaded with salt as though he had come up from the bottom of the sea. For an instant she was painfully aware of his maleness. "Yes, I'm a friend of a friend," he repeated, and let her go.

Eleni smiled, but she did not like the look of this sailor. Inside herself she was not smiling at all.

"You paint here often?" She nodded. "Then there won't be any difficulty. . . . Listen, you look frightened to death. I'm not as barbarous as I seem. Our mutual friend, he talks about you a great deal, and he'll be putting in this way any day. Look for him."

"I don't understand."

"And I can't explain except there's a friend of yours with business in Salonica. Take my word. In a few days he'll be stopping here."

Try as she would, Eleni could extract no more from the sailor. He turned and walked away. Next morning his caique was gone, as though it had never been. Eleni was uneasy. Was she involved in some secret conspiracy? A week passed. November came, with a north wind blowing spray from the waves up to the little cafés. The tables were moved inside and the glass door was shut. In the small rooms, the air was fogged with tobacco smoke and burning olive oil. As the wind rose, the salt spray dusted the roofs until the tiles became encrusted with tiny diamonds. Eleni moved her canvas back to the Hellenic theater and painted from there. The waves fell against the shore with the muffled thuds of falling logs, and the spray sifted down. The sea came from the north, a gray winter sea, and the waves were melted ice. It would be no good in Piraeus until spring, she decided, but because of the sailor she kept on returning. Then came a second message, this time relayed through the waiter Brooklie. He seemed as perplexed as she. "This sailor, you should have seen the way he carried his hands. Like this, you know?"

"I know, I know. What did he say?"

"He said he was a friend of yours, or a friend of a friend of a friend. Something like that. He said things had gone wrong, and not to expect to see anybody until after Easter. I couldn't make much out of it."

"Neither can I," said Eleni, but she felt relieved just the same. Who could it be, this friend of a friend? Surely not Raphael. Secrets and conspiracies were not his way. And it was not like Phaethon to have anything to do with boats. At any rate, the worry had been postponed. As she walked to the station that evening, the lights of Piraeus looked gay, and everything old and used up was hidden by shadow or made softly beautiful. The train itself was packed with commuters swaying together, and it smelled of tobacco and sweat. "I won't think about it until spring," she assured herself, but on hearing the insistent slap, slap of sandals on the platform, her heart beat fast. She tried to turn, but the train was too crowded. The automatic doors were closing.

Eleni did not return to Piraeus that autumn. She confined her painting to the labyrinthian streets of the Plaka but went more often than her professor knew to the Acropolis. When evening came, as it did earlier each night, she would accompany Andreas down from the summit. Sometimes they talked about the Acropolis; she of its beauty, he of the tourists he had met there. More often they were concerned with his contest with the road. "Easy there, that's it," he would say, and on the smooth stretches, "You wouldn't think a man could make it on this thing, day after day." There was a hint of pride in his voice. "You know, these roller skates have real ball bearings. From America. They're like me, they don't give out." Occasionally he even spoke of her painting. "I'll give you fifteen drachmas for that canvas to patch the north window," he would say jokingly. "You know I've never been much on art, but I knew an artist once. One of the modern ones who used to throw great globs of paint on a canvas and then drag a naked woman across it. I mean it. Well, I told him I'd like to clean his brushes. That's as close as I've ever come to art." However tortuous the path, however poor his business, Andreas's face was always full of life and enthusiasm. Eleni could not help liking him, which made her feel the more guilty for the way she conspired to avoid him.

As autumn turned to winter with its bruised gray skies, a cutting wind sang over the stones of the Acropolis. Eleni grew used to Andreas and his cart, to their battle with the path, and to the loungers at the Drunken Boat who hailed him, "Here comes that avalanche! A thousand laughs and twenty fights to the barrel! Andreas!" And he would shout back, "Tempt not the foul fiend to his damnation!" She knew he must yearn to spend the damp evenings there, drinking with his friends in the glare of light and the clatter of glasses. He told her, "Eleni, it's a blind alley," and added rather wistfully, "but it's cozy and comfortable."

The evening came when he stopped in, "for old time's sake." He was back before supper, but Vasso stared at him across the table with only her eyes alive, and they were full of torment. "All right, all right," he said. "I'm a vile old bum fallen among princesses. . . . But let's not start on that." After a while, he did not always return for supper. Eleni said nothing about it the first time she ate alone with her aunt. Vasso said nothing either, until one night when supper was over she asked Eleni to bring him home.

"Why not you, Aunt Vasso?"

"Because he would only make a joke in front of his friends. You'll have more influence. He wants to make a good impression on you. Will you, please?"

It was cold in the house, colder still outside, but Eleni went. The taverna radiated light and warmth. On the steamed windows someone had lettered "EOKA." Inside, the café reeked of wine and beer, onions and shish-kebab. Barrels ringed the walls and under their spouts the floor was puddled. When they noticed her, the customers turned in their chairs. "A Nereid," said one. Then Andreas came rolling without protest.

"It's a good warm place," he said.

"There's a lot of wine, all right," she replied. Privately she had to admit it was a good place for a man like Andreas. And that night when she lay in bed with the wind traveling down from the north, it seemed a good place for anyone. She wondered if the wind that stirred her room would soon be swaying the tall cedars of Troodos, carrying snow to the peaks, puffing out the sail of Raphael's boat. It would be a warmer, gentler wind in Cyprus.

Cyprus was never far from her mind. The radio shrieked constantly of freedom and blood. The English were wicked imperialists, the Turks were the chauvinists of Ankara, and always there was news of the trial. Stephanides Diakos was a household word, a martyr in the Greek world. Eleni pictured him moving symbolically between two rigid soldiers, the three of them interlocked with steel wrist bands, the way Christ had moved before Pilate spoke to the mob. She seemed to see the massive machinery of British law turning, digesting, sifting, moving imponderably toward the inevitable conclusion. It would come, the newspapers said in two-inch headlines, but there would be a price.

That was the dark side of Cyprus. There were also the letters. Her mother wrote encouragingly and spoke of improved health—she would be well by summer. But her father's letters were somber. Demeter was worse, business was poor. His only enthusiasm seemed to be for Phaethon, whose name was becoming known and respected. Should EOKA win, he would have a place in the government. A marriage with him would save the family's health and fortune. Such letters aroused her sense of duty, like ill-fitting shoes that pinched at every step. They forced her to consider her shortcomings, her failure even to hint at her intention of staying on in Athens when summer came.

A letter had even come from Raphael. It was particularly dirty around the stamp, as though it had passed through many hands, but it was the letter Eleni read over again and again. It gave her pleasure to picture Raphael's tongue pushed against his upper lip with the effort of writing, and to feel his independence in the wild stormy handwriting that seemed like the uncontrolled waves of the sea. In content the letter was short and entirely personal; it might have been written by a ten-year-old boy with a sense of humor and no gift for spelling. He had been to Famagusta and back. The *Nereid* had been damaged, though he didn't say how, and now he was on the beach, waiting for better weather. It bothered Eleni that the *Nereid* might be beyond repair. At the last he had mentioned the possibility of building another boat. There was no word of a trip to Athens, and he did not seem the sort to conceal such an adventure. Yet she knew no one else who had to do with the sea.

Huddled over a small kerosene stove, she would write home, passing her loneliness on. She had no address for Phaethon, so she sent him her love in care of Raphael.

At the same time she spoke to Vasso about getting a job. Vasso did housework for two British families near the English school. They directed Eleni to an American family. For three days a week they would pay her well. They also showed an interest in her paintings.

Eleni was to start work the first week in February, but she came down with the flu. It was particularly severe because her body was not used to the wintry climate. Vasso called it a donkey cold. Eleni went to work anyway, but the Americans sent her home with a bottle of pills, which she didn't take. The following week she felt better and went back to work. It seemed to Eleni that, if not as a painter, at least as a housekeeper she had a future in Athens.

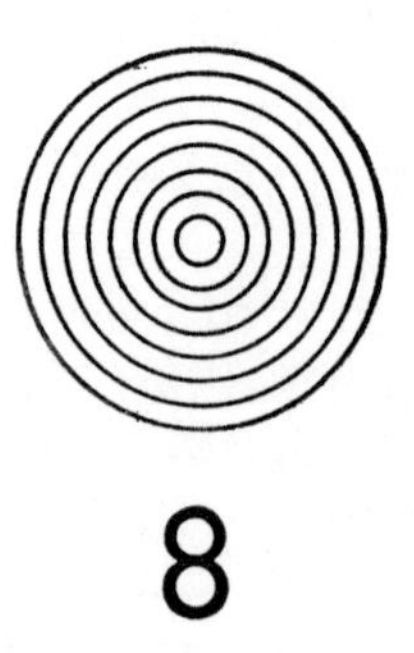

8

Spring made a treacherous appearance. In the Plaka, it sprouted from the manholes. Eleni once again took the subway to Piraeus, and as she disembarked, she was surrounded by the beggar children who in summer masked their poverty by selling flowers. In winter they simply disappeared. Now they waylaid her with outstretched palms. Though she could ill afford it, she gave in to their pleading.

Tourkolimano had not changed. It still bore an autumn look. In the bay, a dowdy tug with a smokestack like a tall black candle slogged against the waves, which rolled from the north. Sighing from the effort, its whistle spouted a milky jet of steam toward the low-flying clouds. Yes, she thought, it is good to be back. Not hesitating this time, she set up her canvas and with a poise and speed of brush which she had not long possessed began to sketch the moving tug. She kept at it doggedly until her right hand began to cramp around the brush. Impatiently she flexed the hand and went to the café for an early lunch.

All the tables were still crowded inside and steam masked the windows. She hailed Brooklie with affection. There was no empty table and she would not intrude on a group of men. It was condescending enough that she was allowed to eat there at all. Finally Brooklie found her a chair near the kitchen and brought her a plate of spaghetti, floating in lukewarm olive oil, which she held in her lap. Overhead the radio was blaring the latest jazz hit from America. It was too noisy, the waiter too busy, for real conversation. However, he managed a word or two above the din. "He's been here again"—with a platter of moussakas. "Every week or so"—returning to the kitchen with a napkin full of fish bones. "Strange sort, doesn't say much"—popping out again with two bottles of retsina and a corkscrew. "Keeps his own counsel, as they say." She hadn't asked, and she wasn't glad to hear the news. Outside again, the slap of every passing sandal brought her eyes up sharp and her heart along with them.

All afternoon she listened for sandals. The following day meant housework, and the day after that it rained. Sandals were still on her mind the next day as she painted in Piraeus, so she was completely unprepared for the hushed approach of bare feet which she saw planted before her easel. They were broad feet, with toenails as dark and horny as tiny turtles. Swiftly her gaze traveled over the worn khaki trousers, the homespun woolen shirt, to the penetrating face.

"Miss Eleni, you've been away."

"What is it you want of me?" she demanded.

"I told you. I'm a friend of a friend."

"And what's that supposed to mean? If you can't explain, why don't you leave me alone?"

"I don't mind telling you because we're the same people, come thick or thin." The sailor leaned toward her, speaking rapidly, his eyes shifting from side to side. "We've had lines out for a long time. Connections in Salonica that got twisted up. Now that it's spring, you'll see something." He clapped her lightly on the shoulder and rocked back on his naked feet. "Yes, indeed."

"Well, go on. What will I see?"

"You'll see a friend. Easter Monday. Top of Lycabettus. He says you can count on it this time."

"All right. What friend?"

"Phaethon. We have a job in Salonica. Supplies. I don't mind telling you we'll have a surprise for Cyprus."

"I don't believe you."

"God's truth! Be at Lycabettus."

"Do you mean Phaethon's getting arms for EOKA?"

"You said that, miss," said the sailor, rocking back, his dark face aglow with holiness conferred by secrecy. "Just remember this. If you give away one word of what I've said, I'll make a corpse of you."

"Don't worry, I'd never report a thing like that."

"What sort of thing would you report, Miss Eleni?"

"Nothing said between friends."

"Swear on the Greek flag you won't mention anything you've heard from me. Swear!" And Eleni swore. With this the sailor slipped off quickly, as though practiced at getting away speedily and silently on bare feet. From a skiff he made his way to an anchored caique. He heaved at a small windlass, the anchor appeared against the side, and the waves began to sweep the boat toward the shore. Then he dashed back to the engine room and the caique turned slowly into the waves. Apparently he sailed alone.

Eleni couldn't paint after that. The thought of seeing Phaethon, the knowledge that he was smuggling guns distracted her completely. His coming should have given her pleasure, but it didn't. She wanted to be alone, to think. Near the station, the beggar children accosted her as usual. She tried to push through them. One had brought his baby brother in his arms. "Look," he muttered, "he's grown a beard. My brother is only three and hunger has put a beard on his face." The children crowded about her.

"Give me fifty drachmas, please."

She walked a few paces.

"Twenty drachmas."

"No money today."

They yelled after her. "Three drachmas! A cigarette!"

Finally she reached the crowded solitude of the subway. She would not return to Piraeus. The next day, perfidious spring crept back into the sewers. Winter returned with raw gusty winds from Macedonia. A cold rain wilted the tender leaves and drove the beggars underground.

With the first days of Holy Week, Eleni felt a stirring of excitement in the air. It was more than the rituals and processions, more than spring. The Athens radio was momentarily expecting the court's decree in the murder and sedition trial of Stephanides Diakos, and the young men of the city were prowling in crowds.

On Passion Thursday, Vasso began the day with a glass of vinegar in honor of Christ's last thirst. Looking outside at the sunshine, she promised, "It won't last," put on one of her three black dresses, and departed. She moved down the narrow street with that forward leaning walk that made her look eighty. Eleni and Andreas soon followed. They took the path to the Acropolis.

It no longer bothered Eleni to accompany her uncle. Sympathy had overcome her embarrassment. She wanted to help by giving a push or removing a stone from his path, but this morning when she threw a small stick aside his great shoulders grew stiff with pride.

"Don't ever do that," he rumbled. "I don't want anyone's pity."

"I'm not pitying you."

"You're a liar. I can see it in your face."

Finally she said, "You shouldn't have to push that thing over all these sticks and stones."

"Don't help me," he said in a very soft voice. "Get out of the way, or I'll run over you."

They went a distance in silence, Eleni walking behind. Andreas seemed to be struggling against his innate friendliness. When he turned half around, his dark sweet eyes were full of a sort of bravado. "Listen," he told her. "Have you ever heard of Sysiphus? He was damned to hell, and he had to keep rolling a great stone uphill, and as soon as he got it to the top, the stone always rolled back. He had to do it over and over, forever, but as long as he didn't give up and didn't give out, he was all right. He had a kind of job and he had his pride. Well, I'm no worse off than anyone else as long as my arms are strong. Don't worry, they won't give out, and if they did I'd pull myself along by my front teeth."

The wind was dry and whistling on the Acropolis. Spring lay below, but up there it was still the March wind they called the Flayer.

Few tourists came that day. Was it the wind, she wondered, or the excitement in the city? She could see in the streets a glimmer of scarlet and white, and she imagined the processions moving to the churches. Back home during

Holy Week girls twined ribbons in their hair, moistened and bit their lips to make them pink, and went out for a stroll. Little boys filled Easter egg shells with gunpowder and used linen thread for fuses. Eleni had not expected to be homesick, but it was hard not to be in Cyprus during Holy Week, when iris and poppies would be coming out along the roadsides. It was hard, too, because she had received another letter from Raphael. In it he spoke of a new boat he was building and he hoped she would come home soon. Otherwise the letter told her nothing of the things she had wanted to know. Still, she brooded over it. She brooded too over the coming of Phaethon. His caique must be very near, somewhere just below the horizon. She would try to meet him on Lycabettus, of course, but it bothered her that she was not altogether eager for his coming.

By afternoon the crowds seemed thicker in the streets, particularly concentrated in Omonia and Constitution squares. She seemed to hear them chanting, "Cyprus, Cyprus!"

She spoke to Andreas, asking whether he had heard any news from the tourists who bought his souvenirs and cards. "No radio, no gossip. To be completely indifferent to the fate of the world is the finest medicine a man can give himself," he said.

"I knew him," she said.

"You mean Diakos? Yes, you said so."

"Everyone in Cyprus must be praying for him now. Whatever happens, he'll be remembered as a hero."

"A misguided little boy," he admonished her. "All the misguided little boys are jangling the keys to the kingdom. Listen to them down there, overturning taxis, breaking glass. They ought to be playing with blocks." She must have looked astounded, for he added, "Maybe my patriotism's a little warped. It's something I ate . . . ten years ago."

During Holy Week in Athens, the theaters and motion-picture houses showed only religious plays and films. Before every neighborhood butcher shop hung the slaughtered lambs for the Sunday feast, heads down so the blood would run from the mouths. It would be the same in Cyprus, with the congregations gathering around open-air pulpits to hear the priest read, "What have they done with my Lord?" And the congregation would shout back, "He is not here. He is risen. *Christos Anesti!*" Then would come the fireworks. From the sounds of tumult below, it sounded as though the last ritual of Holy Week had already begun.

Eleni did not want to find out what was going on. On the way home, she went so slowly that Andreas outdistanced her. She saw him next rolling out of the house, grimly silent and determined, heading for the Drunken Boat.

In the house, Vasso sat alone, arms folded tight across her body, hunched forward as though in pain. She did not speak and there were angry spots of color on her ordinarily colorless cheeks.

"Do you feel like talking?" ventured Eleni.

Surprisingly, Vasso was anxious to unburden herself. Stephan had been condemned to hang. The news was unhappy, but Eleni had never really expected otherwise: this was the reason for the rioting. Vasso had been in the main streets. Trolleys were overturned, and they were British-owned. The dining room at the Acropole Palace Hotel had been wrecked because the crew of a British plane had lunched there. Mobs had burned off the bronze name plaques on the Grand Bretagne Hotel, and there had been riots in the Piccadilly Café until the sign had been changed to "The Cyprus."

"They bombed the British language school," explained Vasso. "It isn't safe being English any more. My people . . ."

"What about your people?"

"They're leaving. They're closing up their houses."

No more had to be said. Vasso was out of work. Andreas had not returned, and they ate in silence. When he finally came rolling up the ramp, he brought the gusty smell of the taverna with him. His face shone as though polished with an oily rag.

"Well, here I am, what's left of me. The rest of me's—well, to the devil with the rest of me." Making a foolish expression, he allowed his tongue to creep out, pointed and glistening, until it all but touched the tip of his nose.

"You've been drinking a little," said Eleni. It was a relief to have him back, however false his gaiety might be.

"No," he waggled his finger, "I've been drinking a lot. Woman of the house, may I trouble you for a glass of wine?"

"Go to bed," Vasso told him. "We have enough troubles."

"Woman of the house, I'm concerned—I'm deeply worried. Does that reassure you? I wouldn't want to be quoted, but the sky is falling. A piece of it seems to have fallen on my legs, and I can't find them."

This got him the wine and he poured a sloshing glass, threw back his head, and downed it in one long draught, with the sound of an emptying bath.

"I'm in bad shape," he announced loudly.

"You certainly are."

"What's a job? You always complained about it. Now you have time. You can be like Eleni. You can paint. Transport yourself." He laughed loudly, his head swaying to and fro. Vasso looked terribly angry and muttered as he laughed, "Oh, that's nice. That's very nice."

"That's her tortured-animal look," said Andreas with a leer.

Eleni, embarrassed, stood apart, assuming as best she could the air of an official mourner at a funeral.

"Woman of the house, I beg you to free us momentarily from your suffering while I have a chat with your niece."

In the deadlock of wills between husband and wife, Andreas proved the stronger. Vasso moved backward to the door, opened it, and was gone.

"I think I can hear her talking outside," said Eleni.

"Forgiving God for bringing her into such a world with such a man, I dare say. I hate her sanctimonious suffering." His voice was loud. "I'm sorry, Eleni. We'll be very quiet now. Very quiet. . . . We're going to have a chat, you and I, and I'm going to get down on my knees—figuratively, of course—and ask you a favor. But first there's a story to tell. This story is about a young hero born into the iron age to restore the age of gold. This was a giant surrounded by ants, and heaven had reserved for him the most dangerous and glorious adventures. This young giant wanted everyone to carry a flag and spear and to sing marching songs, so he became a cadet in the military academy. He was an officer in the great war. With his own pistol, he executed three deserters. He thought the flag was a very important thing, not just a bit of colored cloth, and one day with his foolish little gun he attacked an armored car . . . well, the major came and promised him a medal. That major was comical. 'It isn't so bad, old man. You'll be all right. Everyone respects a man with a limp.' " Andreas uttered a wild sad laugh that stopped as abruptly as it started. "That's where the fairy story ends. While the hero was waking up, somebody stole his legs. His government was appreciative, oh yes. He got a fine brass medal and a kind of job. He was an official hero of the great war, but who remembers that war? They're all too busy on the next one. Eleni . . . I suppose I'm annoying you with all this because of what's going on outside, and because I'm a little drunk and haven't the courage to say what I should. I'll get there—but first I just want to mention another hero, the first hero's brother. You know he ran away from dive bombers, and he thought this was such a cowardly thing to do that he lay down under the almond trees at Kalamata and died of shame. Funny, the best almonds in Greece came from Kalamata. They still do. I can't eat one without thinking of your father and how he's always blaming himself for not charging an armored car like his foolish brother. I never wrote him about the legs, you know. Eleni, are you still listening?"

"You said you never wrote him about . . . them."

"I was ashamed of being a cripple. Then it had gone on so long I was ashamed of being ashamed. But I've found out something about life, I think. It doesn't need heroes or philosophers because it isn't a matter of the end justifying the means. Eleni, there are no ends, there's just living, and it can be simple and magnificent. If you're lucky and you wake up early enough, you don't cripple yourself attacking armored cars because of some notion of heroism. You don't shoot deserters; the world has room for cowards. I like to think the world's still large enough for people to look after themselves, and not interfere with one another, no matter how good and noble their intentions. I've come to believe that even in the hands of a saint the golden rule's an imposition."

Eleni felt uneasy. If there was logic in her uncle's opinions, she had lost track of it, and the room seemed so thick with kerosene smoke that she could scarcely breathe. "If he were not a cripple, he wouldn't speak so bitterly," she told herself unhappily.

"Shouldn't I find Vasso?" she asked.

"Eleni, wait a minute. I'm about to go against everything I've said. That's why I'm having a hard time. I'm about to impose. You've been with us six months or more. But now you know what these years have been like for us. We've been buried alive. Why do you think my wife wears black? She hasn't any dead relatives—only me."

"It must have been terribly painful."

"Yes, but don't you see? To shut out pain, you must shut out everything. It may not show, but Vasso and I depend absolutely on one another, and what I have to say is for both of us." His voice rose softly and earnestly, a manly voice, but he looked like a cornered bull. "Eleni, I don't make much. My income wouldn't feed a sparrow. Now my wife's out of work. Jobs aren't easy to find, and I'm not pretending you don't need work. Eleni . . ."

"You want me to give Vasso my job?"

"Yes."

"What will I do?"

"You may have to go home . . . in time. Perhaps you'll find another job. You're younger, better to look at than Vasso."

She was not surprised at the request, only that it had come from Andreas. She was not even particularly upset. She asked only for a little time to think.

"Thank you," he replied with dignity, as though he knew her decision already. "I'm going to bed. Don't wake me in the morning. I may be dead."

Eleni sat in her room. She could not sleep. Of course she would have to give Vasso her job, but then what? Her thoughts went round and round like mice in a wheel, and she yearned for a beach where green waves were beating, where someone could tell her whether to laugh or cry. She began a letter to Raphael. It was not entirely a question of a job any more, but whether she would be going home. The question was simple, but she was not sure of the answer. It would be wrong to let Athens drive her away. Before the letter was finished, her mind was made up. When Raphael's boat was damaged, he rebuilt it because the sea was his way of life. Art was hers. She would stay and paint, and try to sell her paintings. If her paintings would not sell, she would look for another job. She would beg in the street if need be. Eleni felt close to tears as she finally lay down. "I may be an awful fool," she told herself aloud, "but I'm going to stick it out."

On Easter Monday, Eleni approached the base of Lycabettus with a picnic basket on her arm. Rock-strewn and heavily wooded, it was the place for Phaethon all right, as much like Troodos as Athens could possibly be. Eleni rested not far from the summit. She had just assured herself that he would not come when a voice behind her commanded, "All right, don't move! I've got you covered!" A volley of laughter followed, which she recognized as she had not recognized the voice.

"You! That's not funny! It isn't funny, Phaethon!"

There he stood, tall, handsome, radiant with well-being.

"You don't seem very pleased to see me, Eleni."

"You haven't given me much chance to seem anything. Honestly, what a greeting."

"You look good, Eleni. But why the braided hair? If I were younger, I'd pull it. . . . You do, you really look fine, pigtail and all." He looked at her in a way every young girl wants to be looked at.

"Kiss? Eleni?"

He embraced her. With the pressure of his body, she felt a more sinister impact, hard and metallic, the gun he wore beneath his jacket.

"I've missed you," she said, but the words were no sooner out than she realized she hadn't really missed him at all.

"Do you love me?"

"A little."

"Don't tease, Eleni. How much time do you have?"

"A little while."

"I like the looks of that picnic basket. Come on, let's find a private place to sit down. You've time for that." He took her hand, warmly laced fingers with her.

He picked up the basket and they moved toward the thicker trees. Phaethon walked as though there were springs in the toes of his shoes, yet he made no sound in the dry litter or stumbled over the skeleton hard roots. Here the sun was dimmed. He held Eleni close to him.

"Isn't it beautiful?" Eleni tried to speak impersonally, to reassure herself.

"It's safer," he replied.

"I mean Athens, the Acropolis."

"It's the citadel of the world, but I feel more at home in a town I can walk out of in a few minutes."

"Where can we sit?"

"Oh, here I guess, anywhere—or what about over there?" This too she found beautiful, but Phaethon did not simply sit. He walked round and round, peered and poked before at last sitting down.

"I hate to admit this," he said, "it's not the least bit romantic, but I'm dying of hunger. Do you mind if I see what you've brought?"

He began to inspect the contents of the basket. Bread, soft cheese, three bottles of Fix lemonade. "Is this chicken? You're wonderful." His smile of appreciation was so genuine, so dazzling that she blushed. "You can't imagine the food I'm used to. None at all, mostly, and what we do get is wormy, the meat all green and blue like a rainbow. And that caique! It stinks of fish."

"What about the caique, Phaethon? You're smuggling arms in it, aren't you?"

"I thought Stelios told you about all that."

"The sailor with the black . . ."

"Curly hair all over. That's him. Yes, we've been trying

for arms. I would have seen you last fall, but we lost the caique."

"Sunk?"

"Police took her. Right near the beach." He cut another slice of bread and spread cheese on it. "It's been close to a year since you helped me out with that message, Eleni. They picked me up with a wagonload of onions. Lord, my poor eyes, riding all the way to the Troodos buried in onions. It's been one narrow scrape after another. Well, anyway, all that's safely past."

"I'm glad you're here safe." Eleni looked up, caught his frown, and said, "Why are you looking like that?"

"Oh, it's not you; I was thinking."

"Go on."

"Well, you mentioned the caique, and I began thinking about Raphael. Eleni, he baffles me. I just can't make him out. Do you know we offered him money to dive for some of the old mines? The ones that were put offshore during the war? He wouldn't. He wouldn't help pilot our caiques, either. Who'd have thought we'd end up on different sides?"

"You're not on different sides. Raphael hasn't taken sides at all."

"Like it or not, he's in it. Eleni, just having that no good Turkish friend, that Jamal—that's enough to put him in up to his neck."

"I thought Jamal had gone to Larnaca."

"The damage is done, just the same. Even before this trouble, I never liked that Turk. Always hiding behind Raphael, always leeching off him. There must be something wrong with Raphael, making that kind of friend. Was he dropped on his head when he was a baby? I don't know, but he's an odd one."

"I like him. I like him very much. I don't want you to get angry at Raphael." But there had always been an underplay of friction between the two boys, a friction that she knew she must have promoted simply by being the loadstone that brought them into contact.

Phaethon filled his mouth with a large slice of bread and one of cheese and began to chew rhythmically, his eyes directed at a space somewhere just in front of Eleni.

"He's not like you, Phaethon. He hasn't any anger in him."

"No patriotism, you mean."

"He doesn't want to hurt people."

"Do you think I want to hurt people? I don't want to hear any more about him."

Eleni dipped grapes in the lemonade. Their dark blue skins gathered crusts of little pearls.

"Listen, you're with me now! Are you still thinking about him?" Phaethon demanded.

"No . . . I don't know."

"Tell me what you're thinking."

"Stop it, Phaethon. You act as if you're jealous."

"Certainly I'm jealous of what I don't understand. Anyone would be—it's like having him here. When I count, there's you and me, but I keep feeling there's three of us sitting here."

Eleni looked at him, sturdy and formidable in his forest garb. It was like eating lunch with a stranger. Whether the stranger was Phaethon or herself, she could not decide.

Abruptly he burst into boyish laughter. This had saved him before in many a tight situation, and Eleni recognized it as conciliatory. "I think you're getting angry with me," he said. "Don't be."

She looked at him.

"Smile then . . . good. Eleni?" He was looking at his hands. "I don't mention Raphael to make you unhappy. I wanted to tell you something for his own good. I'm sure you heard what happened to his boat."

"I heard he was building a new one. Tell me, Phaethon, what did happen?"

"It was destroyed, Eleni."

"That lovely old boat . . ."

"He'd been asked to pilot the supplies, you see. There isn't anyone who knows the coves along the western coast like Raphael, and he would have been paid well." But in the hands of a confused pilot the caique had been taken by the British patrols and Raphael, for his refusal to assume the job, had been placed on the EOKA blacklist. "He was lucky it was only the boat that blew up."

"Blown up! Phaethon, how could you do that?"

"I didn't, Eleni, but I couldn't stop it, either. At least he's in one piece, but he can't sit back any longer. He'll be killed. You've got to talk to him. Write him a letter or something . . ." It was as though he were wearing one of the masks that boys wear at Christmas. He seemed concerned, worried, yet there was cruelty in his eyes, a twist to his mouth that she tried to persuade herself was a trick of light and shadow. "Dighenis has left it up to the district leader to make the decision."

"The one you're afraid of?"

"He's gone, Eleni. Last month Dighenis put me in charge of the Paphos district."

"You're joking!" One shock after another brought an increasing sense of unreality. She wanted him to laugh and admit the joke, but his face expressed the most formidable calm. He was deadly serious. He's gone mad, she thought, but looking at the physiognomy across from her she was obliged to dismiss the notion of ordinary lunacy. "Phaethon, last time you said you were staying in EOKA only because you were afraid of the district leader. Now he's gone. Why don't you get out? Why?"

"Maybe you're not supposed to believe what people say," Phaethon replied. He began rolling a cigarette, but his fingers weren't steady. The tobacco kept spilling on the ground.

"But being so irresponsible with other people's lives! Raphael never hurt anyone."

"Eleni, it's my life too. I've said more to myself over and over than you can ever say. I've called myself an assassin. Sometimes when I'm depressed I feel like waiting for the English to come with their dogs. I'm ready to run out on the road and give myself up, and then I think of Stephan."

"You could hide somewhere. You wouldn't have to go back."

"Hide! I'm in too far for that. Let me tell you about the district leader and how he got out of EOKA. One day he was told to shoot a man. It turned out to be an old friend, so he broke his rifle on a tree and sailed to Cos. He had relatives there. He was safe with his own people. At least he thought so, until one morning some shepherds found him. He was in a field full of flowers, Eleni, but all around, the ground was black, scorched. He'd been burned alive in petrol. Listen, when Dighenis suggests, you act. You don't think about it, you do it. Or you disappear. I've killed for him. Yes, Eleni, I have."

Eleni was horrified. "You sound as if you enjoyed it."

"Do I really sound that way?"

"Yes. Oh, Phaethon, what's happening to you?"

"I've wondered sometimes," he admitted unwillingly. "But, Eleni, believe this. If there was any other way to Enosis than fighting, I'd take it."

At last he had managed to fashion a scraggly cigarette. Its smoke hung in bluish whorls above them.

"This isn't easy for me. I can't protect Raphael much longer. You've got to get in touch with him."

"I've never been able to persuade Raphael to do anything. You know how he is."

"He's fond of you, Eleni. Just try again."

"If you can only give him time to finish his boat, he'll leave Cyprus."

"Finish his boat!" exclaimed Phaethon. "He hasn't even started. He hasn't anything to start with, not even money. He justs sits on the beach. We'd pay him good money, Eleni, we still would, but he likes being a sitting duck. He's in your hands, Eleni. If you can't persuade him, he won't be alive next autumn."

"You'd have him killed! Your oldest friend!" The very thought left empty all the years between them.

"No, but I told you before, I don't know how long I can prevent the others from killing him."

"Couldn't you help him along with the boat? The two of you, like old times? Then you could both get away." Eleni knew as she spoke that her words were mere fancies.

"I don't always regret being in EOKA. I know what it stands for is right. I only regret the methods the English and people like Raphael impose upon us." Phaethon no longer sat quietly, but prowled back and forth, back and forth, as though the tall trees were confining bars. "I wish you could meet Dighenis."

"I saw him once," she replied, "in the beginning."

"He's nothing to look at. Small, with a little mustache, and the worst teeth. Sometimes we have to kidnap dentists —but that's not the point. There's steel in him, Eleni. Steel and gunpowder. And he has a way of putting them into us." As Phaethon talked, it seemed to Eleni that his nose pinched in, his ears moved back along his skull. She sat quietly. This was no time for her to speak. "Once when the English were after him, he spent five weeks hiding in a dark little hole up to his ankles in water. There's a story he once disguised himself as a beggar to shake the hand of the English governor. Eleni, there's no one like him."

Eleni had the feeling that Phaethon's words were not really addressed to her, but were part of a long internal reverie.

"I believe he hates this awful killing as much as I do, but he knows it's the only possible way and he's the only possible leader. He can get the best out of every one of us. When he gets us together and speaks of Enosis, sparks seem to shoot out of him. Even if I could speak like him, I couldn't begin to give you an idea of how we feel. He puts up with more hardship than any of us and he doesn't complain, never. When I get discouraged he talks to me as though he hadn't anything better to do. My father never bothered, but he does. That's why I could never let him down. Never."

"If he were caught, what would happen?"

"It would mean the end for all of us. That's why it mustn't happen." Phaethon's face was somber, not with self-doubt, but with the darkness of one dedicated to a desperate and vital enterprise. "I would follow him to hell." However hard he may seem, I love him and what he stands for. . . . Eleni, I'm frightening you."

"It's just that you've never talked this way before."

"It isn't me you're hearing," Phaethon said. "It's Dighenis talking." But Eleni believed she was seeing Phaethon for the first time, seeing him as someone who might well destroy himself through an excess of wrong-headed zeal. "And the bad times won't last forever. You'll see. When it's over, I'll be somebody in Cyprus."

"I'd rather you were nobody in forestry school."

"Forestry school!" he echoed, as though the idea were amusing. Squatting on his haunches, he mussed up her hair with his fingers. "Soon as it's over, we'll be married. I couldn't do any better than you, Eleni. You're kind and simple. Capable, too . . . make wonderful picnics . . . no onions at all." A broad smile displayed his teeth; regular and white, impersonal as piano keys. "You won't have to do a thing. We'll have servants. You'll be a lady of leisure."

She heard him only dimly. Her father would have regarded this as a good time to mention her mother's welfare, her need for hospital care, but she realized that Phaethon would take such a suggestion as a kind of promise. She sat quietly and tried to smile as he pictured their life together. He simply meant to put her in his pocket, a large and comfortable pocket admittedly, but one in which she would smother.

"It sounds just like the way your parents live."

"Oh, no," he said, "it won't be at all like that. I'm not like my father. He's always complaining because everything has changed. What galls me is that nothing ever changes, not unless you make it change. You can bet your sweet life we're going to, and my British-loving father can go—you know where he can go!"

"Don't bet *my* sweet life," she told him.

"Well, I'm betting mine, sweet or not. I haven't much choice."

Eleni was far too honest to harbor something in her heart for long. She had been exposed to England's great air-conditioned planes. She had lived in the world and had gained a sense of the world's size. It didn't seem possible that a handful of mountain fighters could overcome the will of the British Commonwealth, and she told Phaethon so. "There's no good being right if you're killed for it." Besides, couldn't Cyprus continue to profit from British technology and cultural tradition? She did the best she could to put this into words. There followed a long silence while Phaethon studied her in dumb astonishment.

"You honestly think that," he said. "I'll never understand you, Eleni."

"That's what I'm afraid of," she admitted. "But don't look like that. I may laugh . . . you look so comical. Seriously, Phaethon, I want to tell you about my uncle in Athens. He used to be like you."

But Phaethon wasn't a patient audience. "Listen," he said, "the English may win the battles, but the war will go on, and they'll die with their hands full of victories."

What battles, what war, she wondered? There were only murders, assassinations. But Phaethon kept on talking about the struggle on Cyprus and the greater struggle for Greek solidarity. He imagined Turkish and Greek battleships clashing in another Salamis, and his every word seemed to confirm an awful truth, that the goal for which he lived was not real at all, but a terrible and enormous deception.

"We may all of us be crazy," he admitted, as though in response to her thoughts, "but we've come too far to turn back. We've got to press on to Enosis or die trying." He sat silently shaking his head like a bulldog which has set its teeth and will hold on viselike until its head is severed from its body.

"I want to make a treaty with you," she said, "because I think you're getting angry."

"I'm not angry, not at you." Thoughtfully he rolled another cigarette, took a deep draw, and blew out the smoke. Just as thoughtfully he touched the cigarette's red-hot tip to a patch of dry duff. There was no flame at first, only a feather of smoke. "Did you ever see a crown fire, Eleni? It's a magnificent sight. The roar of it! It's hardly a fire at all, more of an explosion from one tree to another, with the pine needles heated so hot they glow like the filaments of electric lights before they burst into flame." The little fire in the leaf mold was visible now, and gnawing slowly into a wider circle. "How hungry it is!" he said, and almost burned his hand as he watched it with wide bright eyes. "Given a dry day and a wind, a little fire like this might flame up two hundred feet. Battalions couldn't stop it, with the right wind. It hasn't any feeling. You can't hurt it."

But fire was blundering and stupid, she thought. It could be killed. "Shouldn't you put that out?" Her voice was calmer than she felt.

Phaethon poured dirt on the little fire, saying, "One day, we may not put it out, Eleni."

"How could you burn all the lovely trees? Think of the animals."

"If it meant Enosis, I would turn Cyprus into a cinder. Every one of us would, willingly. That's how it is, but it needn't come to that. If we can get the weapons from Salonica . . . if you can get Raphael to cooperate . . . if we have a little luck . . ."

"I'll do my best," she told him, and so she would. At the same time she felt overwhelming weariness at the thought of the danger to come, of all those who had not yet bled.

The following morning she was up and outside before the others were stirring. Her decision to return to Cyprus, where her living expenses would be assured, had put extra spending money in her pocket, and she had a purpose for it. She went to the Flea Market, the bills clutched in her hand. Through the stalls of used clothes and rusty machinery and moldering icons she searched, until she found what she wanted. It was practically new: a sturdy wheelchair. It would take all the money she had, but it seemed like very little in terms of her great fondness for Andreas.

In the afternoon she had it waiting for him outside the house when he returned from the Acropolis. He arrived thunderously on his tiny wheels, stopped and looked at Eleni, stared at the new vehicle. Not a word was said, at first.

"It's for you," she told him.

"That contraption?" He laughed harshly. "For me?"

"To make it easier going up and down," she explained.

He went right on laughing, then to her horror took hold of the wheelchair with his massive hands and sent it bounding down the street. For a moment his eyes blazed. Then he threw himself sideways on his cart and smashed his fist against the wall.

Eleni walked quickly into the house and up the stairs. Her eyes were wet and burning, but she did not cry. She didn't understand, and she was totally unprepared for Vasso's arrival. There was a radiant fury in her aunt's ugliness, and for a moment Eleni had the expectation of nails in her face.

"We don't want your pity here," said Vasso. "We don't want any superior angel's charity in this house. You won't be satisfied until you sprout wings."

"Did Andreas say that?" asked Eleni.

"He didn't have to say it. He was so humiliated he could hardly speak. If you're so crazy to help people, go home. Be a nurse, get married, but don't interfere with us. Eleni, I didn't come here to make a scene. I'm sure you thought you were being kind, but the kindest thing would be for you to find another place."

"I intend to," said Eleni. "Last night I decided to go home. You can have my job . . . any time." At this news, Eleni hoped for a smile. It didn't come.

"I don't mean to drive you away."

"You haven't. The job's open, that's all, and I'm going."

Eleni now had the initiative. Vasso turned away. She uttered a short dry sob disguised as a cough. "What do you want me to do? I'll go down on my knees if you want me to." The last was uttered fiercely, as though Eleni had demanded such behavior. "I didn't come to ask for your job," said Vasso. Then she squared her shoulders as if her mind was made up. She passed out of the room without another word, but Eleni knew she would take the job, gratefully. Nothing more would ever be said, and they would tolerate one another until the end as though nothing had happened.

Her relationship with Aunt Vasso had never really mattered, but she had grown very fond of her uncle. She wanted to part with him as a friend, but the last days passed quickly and they hardly spoke. When Eleni went to the Acropolis, she went alone. She did not go often. The dawn of her last day in Athens came with rain. She might have packed her paints away had it not been for one last unfinished painting. And she might have finished it there in her room, but the Acropolis still held a great attraction for her; a changed attraction, it was true, but as strong as ever.

Before she had reached the sentinel's post, the rain had ceased. The cloud ceiling, crisscrossed with widening cracks, was lifting steadily along the mountain slopes. By midafternoon, when she had applied the final touch of paint, the sun was bright. She would have lingered until dark, but she was afraid that Andreas would leave without her. He was there beneath the temple of Athena Nike, and she went to him, the painting under her arm.

This was their first deliberate confrontation since the rejected gift.

"I did this for you," she said, and held out the picture.

He took it suspiciously and studied it. Then his face enlarged into a bewildered grin of appreciation. "That's me right there! Hey! How do you speak to a painting? I want to say how I like it."

"It's my best," she said. It was the Acropolis as she saw it now, beautiful as a graceful skeleton; stripped of flesh, bone-white, without life—except for a small figure set upon a cart, a small figure that made all the difference.

"Look," he said, "I'm not going to take this as a gift. It's too good. I'll pay for it."

"No, please. You—" She was about to say, "can't afford it," but she held her tongue.

"I haven't much," he said, "but I've saved a small amount. I sold that metal contraption with wheels, the kind of thing cripples use. So here." He gave her a handful of bills and coins, and she took it without counting.

"Let's go home," he said. "Will you carry this for me, until we get there?"

They were friends again. Eleni felt happy and sad at the same time. She wanted to run, but she kept pace with the cart.

"If I weren't your uncle and an old married man, I'd ask you to marry me, Eleni. I would."

"And I'd be honored to accept," she told him.

They were the last ones to leave the Acropolis. Its long shadow lay across the city, where lights were coming on in the deep streets. Andreas talked to his cart and to the path as he went. "Steady, steady. Keep going . . ." In his descent he seemed complete master of his fate, such as it was. She was sorry for him no longer.

"I shouldn't talk to myself so much," he said. "There's a saying, 'When you are happy, be silent, so the birds of happiness will nest in your hair.' "

They did go the rest of the way in silence. Nothing more needed to be said. Eleni took one backward look at the Acropolis as the final shaft of yellow light touched the columns of the Parthenon. "How wonderful! How wonderful it is," she thought to herself. But it was behind her now. Cyprus lay ahead.

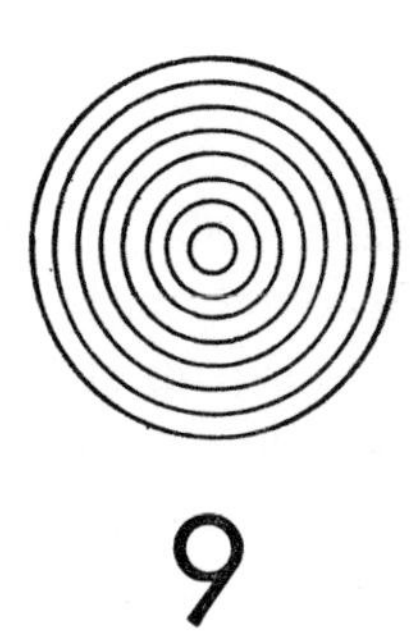

9

The plane went straight out over the Saronic Gulf into the blaze of sunrise. It was too bright to see the islands about which Homer had sung. It was too bright even to look down, for the sea was as dazzling as a polished brass shield.

Eleni felt she might never see Athens again. Far from winning the fame she had dreamed of, she had not sold even one of her pictures. They had all been left with Andreas, who had promised to display them at his stand: huge postcards, too big for stamps, just right for patching north windows. That was all right. She would never regret Athens. She had grown there, grown enough to accept the necessity of going home to prevent a tragedy.

The plane was practically empty. The other passengers looked like government employees; typical colonials concerned with small cars, yacht clubs, and invitations to Government House on the Queen's birthday. This time there were no children. Cyprus must be too dangerous for summer holidays, and Eleni thought of her young friend on her first flight.

As much as she could overhear of conversation was concerned with the hanging. It would take place this morning unless the Governor granted a last-minute stay. Across the aisle sat a man with a dispatch case chained to his wrist. Impressed by this, she tried very hard to listen to his opinions. "Actually," he was saying, "you know there aren't so very many of these EOKA gunmen chaps. I mean, they've proved it ballistically. They say this Diakos is informing on the whole lot of them. Probably thinks he'll get a reprieve."

Eleni sat up straight. Stephan was a hero, a martyr. He wouldn't do such a thing. And yet, why not? His life was at stake, and there wasn't anything glamorous about being a dead hero. She'd learned that much.

Relentlessly the plane droned on toward Cyprus. Too excited to drowse, she closed her eyes against the dazzling light, until the Englishman said, "Dear old cannibal isle . . . there she lies."

Home! The girdling blue-green ocean, the ancient soil rising into dark forests that smelled of perpetual night. Eleni looked upon them with love.

Safety belts were fastened. There was a hiss of decompression as the plane settled, bumped once, and recovered itself. Then came the first delay. For some time the plane sat at the end of the runway, and even when it rolled nearer the administration buildings, its door remained sealed. Finally the boarding ramp arrived, and an announcement was made that the passengers should wait beside the plane.

Eleni emerged into the smothering heat of Cyprian summer. After the air-conditioned cabin, it almost knocked her down.

"This isn't the usual landing place, is it?" she asked a stewardess.

"No. There's a rather noisy crowd around the main building. We've set up customs at a quieter place."

"Noisy crowd?" asked Eleni, though she knew the reason.

"Surely you've heard about the hanging. It's over."

A throng of visitors milled outside the improvised customs shed. Eleni saw her father and ran to him. She felt his dry kiss on her cheek and gave a hard squeeze in return.

"How's mother?" she asked him.

"I don't know, Eleni. I do know she'll be happier when she sees you."

They hurried for the bus.

"I'm not used to this heat," she told him.

The sun seemed to splinter back from the pavement.

While they waited at the bus station, Lazarus inquired about his brother and Eleni replied, "He's fine. He's a wonderful man." Somehow she did not feel entitled to tell the whole story, and her father did not press her. He bought some fried loukmades, and the honey made her thirsty. At a kiosk she found an orange drink and scanned the towering headlines, so tall and black that even an illiterate farmer would be able to interpret their foul meaning. Finally the bus came, dusty, shedding paint, and they boarded while pasteboard suitcases, baskets, and cardboard cartons were dragged up a rusty ladder to the roof.

"Have you seen anything of Raphael?" Eleni asked.

"Not directly. You heard about the boat. Such a pity. Now they say he just sits around the beach and swims and waits for EOKA."

"What do you mean, waits for EOKA?"

"For them to shoot him. Everyone knows he's on their list. Anyone else would defend himself, or more likely, run away."

Because the bus was stifling, a number of passengers waited on the road. The driver shouted at them. "Ladies and gentlemen, does this bus want to go to Paphos tonight?"

They rolled slowly at first, impeded by noisy young men who poked black flags at the windows and would not move out of the way. Once they had escaped the city, the driver shoved in the clutch and shifted violently into second gear. Then he gunned the motor hard and flung it into third, only to apply the brakes so suddenly that Eleni was almost thrown to the floor. "Idiot!" shouted the driver at a bewildered old shepherd, whose henlike fluctuations had nearly been fatal. Again the bus shot forward with a jerk that flattened Eleni against the back of her seat. The plaster icon of Saint George that hung over the driver's seat jogged on its string.

"Raphael's old enough to make his own decisions. He's a grown man. If it weren't for this execution stirring things up. . . . Personally, I never had much use for that Diakos boy. I mean, if they'd gotten him quietly out of the way it wouldn't have been any loss to society. But this trial! You can't imagine the songs and legends they've made up about him. Now there's a rumor that his body won't be surrendered to his mother. It's made things hard at the shop. Eleni, there's a favor I must ask you." Her father seemed to be addressing the window.

"Go ahead, Father. Tell me."

"I can't tell you so quickly. I don't really want to have to ask you at all."

Eleni bit her lips with vexation. "Father, just tell me."

"Your mother's future is in your hands."

"Go on," she urged him, but she felt her own happiness collapsing.

"It's drugs, Eleni."

"And I'm to carry them?"

"Yes."

"To the mountains again?"

"To the monastery. You'll be able to see your mother. Phaethon too."

"I suppose Father Grikos is behind this?"

"Since you had no trouble before, he suggested . . ."

Always coiled at the center of family difficulties seemed to be Father Grikos. Lazarus had no defense against him. Eleni no longer despised her father for this. Perhaps his long-suffering humiliation took a kind of courage after all. Since her mother's welfare depended upon it, she was ready to support him, to be his shield if need be. She turned to tell him so, when a small bundle in colored clothes darted across the road and under the bus.

Brakes and tires squealed and the bus stopped, shuddering, against the wall of a house. The small obstruction slid from the bumper to lie in the road like a pile of empty rags.

People rushed from the houses. The passengers disembarked, forming an ineffectual circle about the felled child. All her life Eleni had cringed at the sight of suffering and she held back, expecting someone with authority to take charge. No one did. The child lay there gasping, eyes wide, too badly hurt to cry. Helplessly the crowd stood by, whispering now, heads inclined almost reverently at what seemed the proximity of death. Someone ran down the sleepy street calling for a doctor, and the voice was shockingly loud. "Mother of God," Eleni demanded of herself, "will no one give him even the comfort of an arm, a word of assurance?" Surely Christ hadn't meant people to live and die alone.

Appalled, she pushed through them to kneel beside the child. She remembered enough of her first-aid classes to know that he was beyond superficial help. She implored the crowd for a doctor, but they stood there seemingly immune to any emotions, until a hysterical woman burst through. With a terrible wail she swooped down and would have cradled the broken child in her arms had not Eleni held her back bodily. That much she remembered. "Don't move him, don't touch him until the doctor comes. . . . Keep the sun off. That's all you can do." So the mother stood between her child and the sun, little shrieks bursting from her with the piercing regularity of a trapped rabbit. "Holy Mother," she cried, "give me back my child and I will give you all our olive trees! I will give you the ox!"

Then the village doctor arrived, a quack with dirty fingernails and magic spells. Relying on the power of its icons, he demanded the child be carried to the village chapel. Eleni barred his way as well, while the crowd took sides, most of them against the young intruder who presumed to contradict the village sage. Finally, as Eleni was about to be forcibly thrown aside, an ambulance arrived. The spectators grew silent, the ring of people distending to admit the English doctor. A stretcher followed and with it a bottle of plasma which the doctor adjusted. Through the eye of a steel needle life began to flow back into the child's body, drop by drop. No longer useful, Eleni withdrew and the crowd closed elastically behind her. Time passed. The spectators began to seek the shade across the street. Beside Eleni on the outskirts of the crowd stood a grave-looking priest. "Po-po-po," he said concernedly. When the doctor called him, he knelt for a moment beside the mother, then accompanied the stretcher back to the ambulance. With the child inside, the ambulance rolled away.

Respectfully the villagers watched its passage out of

town. Then the owners of the house against which the bus was leaning began threatening a damage suit. The bus itself had a flat tire and no pump could be found.

Eleni sat in the shade with her back propped against the wall. Her father disappeared and returned with a loaf of bread and a tin of water.

"These buses are deadly," he said. "We used to get along perfectly well without them."

Otherwise they did not discuss the accident. Lazarus hunched over his bread in silence, then turned a weary face to Eleni and tried to smile. He looked shrunken, suddenly much older.

"Drugs, Father?"

He cleared his throat nervously. "We never did finish our talk. Eleni, if I were the only one involved, I'd never ask this."

"But you're thinking of Mother."

"Yes."

"If Mother were lost somewhere and the police came, how would you describe her to them?"

"What has this got to do . . ."

"I was only wondering."

"Well, she's not very tall. A middle-aged woman with gray hair who looks as though she's been sick . . . very frail."

"Nothing else?"

He was sweating from the sun. His teeth showed. "I guess I don't see your point, Eleni. What about the drugs?"

"Of course I'll take them."

She had nothing more to say, but Lazarus went on unhappily, "It won't be for long. The revolution's going badly. I wouldn't let you do it if I thought there was the slightest risk. Eleni, you believe that, don't you?"

"I believe you, Father."

It was like covering a corpse with flowers, heaps of flowers, but always the corpse was underneath.

Not until late afternoon was the bus repaired. Wearily the passengers crowded aboard. A vendor of caramels squeezed up and down the aisle, and they left with a new driver at the wheel.

The bus, wobbling from a bent axle, arrived in Ktima after dark. Eleni and her father walked home carrying her baggage. Already Athens seemed a half-forgotten dream, and she went directly to her room. There were the same paintings on the walls, the bed made awkwardly by a man's hands, and the long dark mirror from which a weary ghost girl stared out at her. "So you're back again," she told the face, and lay down on the bed. She was too tired even to snuff out the candle.

A sparrow fretting on the window ledge awakened her. She sat up, noticed the puddle of hardened wax, and laughed. Yesterday was over. She did not intend to drag it along with her, but arose and ate and went outside to see if anything had changed. The priest's huge painting of the shield of Achilles stood on its easel beside the chapel: cities in flames, the victors holding their weapons high, a fallen hero borne in deathly triumph. There in paint, some of it still wet to the finger, some cracked already with age, was the song of glory by which she had once been deeply stirred. Now it seemed to her a pious lie to fill up men's heads with the worship of blood and iron. What a thing to hang in a sacred monastery! She knew very well that Father Constantine would never see it hung through choice. Only Father Grikos's influence with EOKA guaranteed its acceptance.

If the painting had been up to her, she would never have created this fierce distortion of Homer. She would replace the fiery reds and blacks with yellow and blue; golden yellow for the sunlight and blue for the sea, with yellow again for sunlight on the water. Those two lovely colors would be enough to portray Cyprus as it ought to be. But it was one thing to paint inside the head, much harder when the paints were taken from the box. Her art would remain the brightest hope of her future, but with Cyprus in turmoil there was little time for painting. There might be no time at all during the ominous summer that awaited her.

As she walked toward the harbor, Eleni picked Adonis flowers, their petals blown out like bubbles of blood. When she arrived, the beach was empty. The fleet was out. Except for a scurry of sandpipers printing the sand with indecipherable messages, there was no sign of life. Disappointed, she was about to leave when she saw Raphael, far out in the marching waves, splashing and snorting.

Most fishermen associated the sea with toil and fatigue and did not play in it. Raphael always had, for there, amid the waste of water and the whipping wind, he felt happy and near to the wild heart of life. She waved, and he shot waist-high, shaking a tiara of water from his hair. Then he stroked toward the beach. Each time he thrust his right arm forward, his body arched above the surface, hard and polished as cedar.

Eleni walked out knee-deep to meet him. She waited as he lunged through the shallows, his limbs glimmering beneath the water like cold green marble.

"Hello, angel," he shouted. "Welcome back to hell. I heard you were coming. Have a good time in paradise?"

"No."

"What did you do?"

"I aged," she told him. "I withered."

"Come on! You look fine." He put out his hand and traced the line of her eyebrow, rubbing it softly against the grain. "This is a good day."

She looked for that old glimmer of gaiety in his eyes

which for her was like the vital spark Prometheus had smuggled from the gods. Now his eyes betrayed him. Between them she seemed to see etched a faint line of bewilderment, despite his free and easy manner.

"You look cold," he told her. "Come on to the beach."

"I heard what happened to your boat. I don't know how to say . . ."

"Poor old *Nereid*. She forgot who she was. She tried to become a bird, but she was too old. She flew up all right, but when she came down she was all in pieces." It was his habit to build up laughter from inadequate materials. There was no laughter now, and he added without pretense, "She burned to the water in an hour. Her keel is down there somewhere now. Good Lebanese cedar, it was. All I've got left is the tiller."

"I thought you'd be more upset."

"It's been a while, Eleni. But there won't be another *Nereid*, not if I live a million years. Sometimes I feel like part of me sank along with her. It's funny, too. Sometimes I wake up in the morning and it's like a mirage. I think I see her moored right out there."

"I wish you'd taken their money, Raphael. You could have used it."

"If they'd offered me twenty thousand pounds, I wouldn't have taken it."

"You must hate them for what they did."

"It was an old and leaky boat." Even now he retained a Franciscan gentleness, which was always the inward expression of his troubles.

"I'd hate them," she told him.

"I know, I know. But that's all done with now."

"It's easier to get over a thing if you talk about it."

"That's not my trouble," he replied. "It's easy enough to get over things. It only seems hard to get on with something else."

"Raphael, I'm frightened for you. They'll try again. You must leave Cyprus. For my sake—the sooner the better."

"Listen, Eleni, before you go any further, I've got a message to deliver from Phaethon."

"You've seen him? He spoke to you?"

"Not directly. He sent me a warning. Even so, he apparently still trusts me. I suppose if it weren't for him I'd have been shot by now. Anyway, he says I'm to listen to you."

"Then you know why I'm trying to get you to leave."

"Yes, Phaethon conveyed the idea."

"Raphael, stay friends with him," she pleaded.

"Whatever can be done by smiling, you may rely on me to do."

"He's important now. They'd have killed . . ."

"No one grows too tall to hang, Eleni . . . or too fast for a bullet."

"Imagine being Stephan. Think of him, yesterday."

"I didn't really know him," said Raphael, "but I felt sorry for him yesterday. I thought what those last few minutes must be like. So vivid. You must notice all the buttons on the soldiers' shirts, the color of their eyes."

"No, it would be an awful blur," she said. "Awful . . ."

"His funeral's today. I don't think the English were wise, handing over his body. The priest will make a show of it."

"I used to love Father Grikos," said Eleni, "but he's an interfering old cow."

"A sacred one, at that."

"He hates you, Raphael. He'd gladly see you dead. So many would."

He smiled. "At night, sometimes, I get panicky, but when it comes round to morning I see another beautiful day. I take a swim. I baptize myself. It's only at night I worry."

"Has nothing else happened?"

"Nothing much. One night there was a shot. It was pitch

dark. I don't suppose it was intended for me, but I was frightened. I don't look behind me any more, not at night."

"But Raphael, how can you just sit here and talk about it?"

"Let's forget it. There's nothing to be done."

"You mean you're just going to sit here like a dead storage battery? Like some kind of target?"

"Go ahead and make a suggestion," he told her. "If I had the money, perhaps I ought to buy a cheap coffin."

"There's only one thing to do. Get away. For heaven's sake, Raphael. You can't just sit here and make stupid jokes."

"If I had a thousand pounds, I'd get a ticket to Hong Kong. If I had fifty pounds, I'd go back to Malta. But I've got one shilling. Anyhow, you know how I like skipping them across the water."

"Haven't you anything at all?" she asked.

"My assets are conspicuously not of this world."

"You're completely broke?"

"To the last shilling," said Raphael.

"Well, don't sound smug about it."

"It's a simple fact."

"Why not get a job in Paphos?"

"I'm on the EOKA list. Who'd give me a job?" said Raphael.

"You could cut your own wood for a new boat."

"I can't risk going into Troodos."

"Doesn't it frighten you to sit here and think about being shot?"

"Nobody gets out of life alive," Raphael replied.

"Suppose you had a boat? Would you go then?"

"I would. If some magician with a magic lamp came and gave me a boat, I would sail away." He looked for a moment into her eyes as if he were penetrating some secret source of hope.

"Have you seen Jamal lately?" Eleni asked.

"No."

"He's working on the salt lake down near Larnaca, isn't he?"

"I suppose so," said Raphael.

"He could get you a job away from here."

"That salt gets under your skin. It gives you leopard spots. I have my calling, Eleni. Besides, EOKA's all over the island."

"All right, what if Jamal comes back? With his help, and mine too, we could fix up some sort of boat."

"You'll be going back to Athens in the autumn."

"I'm home for good."

"Even so, Turks are more unpopular every day. I couldn't bring Jamal back into this danger. I couldn't do that. Don't worry about it, Eleni. If I've run out of luck, it's my business."

"I've heard laziness called bad luck so often that maybe it is," she retorted, but she knew she was not being fair. About Raphael there was an air of unmistakable doom. Sentenced as surely as Stephan, he awaited execution, neither seeking it nor fleeing from it.

Presently Eleni started for home. She had come back to Cyprus to save Raphael, and so far she had achieved nothing. She did not really know where to start. He was still a mystery. He did not seem to be a creature of the past, certainly not of the present, and it was unthinkable that he belonged to the future. He seemed to inhabit a limbo world of his own design, amid drying fish nets, tar, and seaweed. Somehow she would have to reach into this private world and jar him loose, and she knew she had very little time.

At home, she began to write Jamal a letter. It must be dignified, without any of the strain she felt. She must simply ask if it were possible for Raphael to get a job in Larnaca among the Turks in order to earn money to rebuild his boat. Raphael was too proud to write, she said. Otherwise, everything was fine. Through each carefully written word, she could see Raphael sitting on the sand, waiting to be shot.

Eleni had just sealed the letter and was gazing at the address when the chapel bell sounded. The monotonous tolling of the black-tongued deathbell carried the people of Paphos to the little chapel and the old cemetery behind it. She went out of curiosity, and in the knowledge that she would only hurt her friends and family by ignoring the last tribute to an EOKA hero.

It gave her a queer, lonely feeling to see the candles burning in the chapel. The place was already crowded. Latecomers had to stand outside. Before the iconostasis she saw the corpse. Stephan Diakos lay in an especially heavy way, as dead men always do. Wrapped in a clean white sheet, he lay with his hands and feet crossed and tied with twine to commemorate Christ's death.

His big drooping body draped in scarlet, Father Grikos stood before them all, his hands joined upon his breast, his eyes rolled shyly upward as though his soul were already a consecrated sacrament. Finally he raised his swathed, winglike arms, and called for silence. He began to speak in a soothing voice. "You all know why the bell called you this morning. To bid farewell to this beloved boy. Some will say it is a shame and a disgrace to die as he did, but Jesus Christ told us, 'Blessed is he who is persecuted for righteousness' sake.' Saints have been burned at the stake in Cyprus because they would not turn from a righteous cause. It is no different with this boy. Like the saints before him, he has passed through fire to the bosom of God."

His silvery beard jutted out like a stiletto. "Last night I pondered what I should say to you this morning, what comfort I might offer. I found no words." Here he paused and glanced obliquely up at the dim ceiling as though he saw something which was revealed to him alone. "I stood as I am standing now when the roof over my head seemed to split open and I saw . . . I tell you I saw the great flaming eyes of Jesus Christ. I saw those eyes and a huge flaming hand which took me by the arm. Look, can you see the marks?" He held forth his arm. "Those blisters were left by God's fingertips!" His voice volleyed through the small chapel. He struck one clenched fist upon the other. "He has not visited Cyprus with peace, but with a flaming sword. This boy, whose body lies among us, was that sword. In glorious sacrifice he yielded up his life. Others of us must become that sword, and some of us must sacrifice our blood. But if we die as he died, it will be into the hands of God, for whom we fought. How long must this boy's murder go unavenged? How long must we suffer British imperialism and the crimes of the Turkish police? There is only one answer. No longer!"

"Enosis!" someone shouted.

The congregation stirred, ready for bloody deeds.

"As it is written in Isaiah, we must be as the remnant of Jacob, consuming the forests and the fruitful fields with fire to purge them of alien corruption!"

As Father Grikos raved, Eleni slipped outside to get away from his voice, from the air that was too heady with emotion and incense. Presently the priest emerged. In the sunlight, his balding head sprang from his robes with an extraordinary effect of nakedness. She thought of his body, sour and white all over.

He strode at the head of the procession, his arms jerking stiffly like those of a moving corpse. The actual corpse followed, borne by six young men, who held it triumphantly high. The first few paces of the funeral procession seemed more like a victorious march. Then tradition took over, and the women lifted their arms in the air and let out long pure wailing cries. Once again the dead was remembered. The men walked silently except for the sound of shuffling feet, their dark faces inclined with a courteous lack of expression. Lazarus was among them. In years past, he had never had anything good to say about Stephan, but he mourned him now. My father, she thought, with his little shriveled-up soul. How huge and patriotic his mustache had grown! But she followed along for the sake of her mother and Raphael.

In the bright summer midday, the grave filling looked unreal. She could not imagine anyone being dead. Finally it was over. Stephanides Diakos, martyr and hero, was boxed, dated, and hidden under flowers. The crowd, except for a few members of the family, streamed away. Some went to consume the funeral meats with lusty appetites. Others, like Eleni, returned to their homes. A few of the young men went to throw grenades at the British barracks. Most of the grenades failed to go off, and from the others the soldiers escaped, scattering to safety. Only the pregnant wife of a sergeant-major, returning with groceries, was not fast enough.

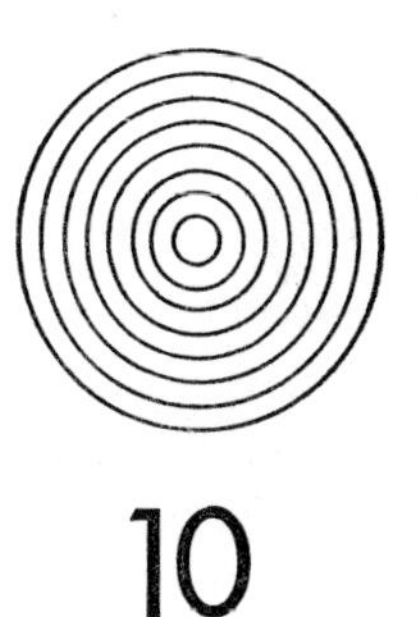

10

June, with its sultry golden days, was over. July brought the days of brass and molten iron, and still Raphael sat on the beach. Eleni's second letter to Jamal remained unanswered. Almost weekly, she ran the line of Troodos sentries with drugs for EOKA. It was an occupation full of horrible probabilities, but she faced the danger with a passionate desire to defend her own: her father, her mother, and Raphael. If only Phaethon would see the gesture as she did, her overt patriotism might be accepted as a substitute for Raphael's indifference.

On her first trip to the monastery, she had again met Father Constantine at the fire station. He stood on the upper platform devouring a box of sesame cakes, like a great shaggy caterpillar munching a cabbage. He looked tired. "I am tired," he had said. "It's that Father Grikos of yours."

"You know him?"

"For my sins. And for his."

As Father Constantine explained it, the two priests had shared a cell years before at Kykko Monastery. Now Father Constantine was in charge of receiving and hanging his colleague's painting. "You know, I really don't approve of that infernal picture at all. So unchristian." However, it was not the painting which wearied him, but Father Grikos's funeral oration and its possible consequences. "It's such a dry summer, Eleni. We lost many men last year, fighting fires. Oh, these EOKA people are as clever as apes. One of these days, they'll roll the earth up into a pellet and swallow it, if they haven't burnt it to a cinder first. Now, with your Father Grikos absolutely giving his endorsement to violence, there's no telling. . . . Do you know him well?"

"I used to think so," she replied.

"You have to know Grikos really well to dislike him. I see no light of God in that man. Still, he goes on forging God's name on every word he utters. Oh, I am tired. . . . Forgive me for saying such things, Eleni. Let's blame it on this mountain of fat meat my soul's obliged to lug about."

Ponderously he had walked beside her while they discussed Demeter. Father Constantine made an admission. "Everything possible is being done, Eleni, but frankly, it's not enough. If she could only be transferred to some really modern clinic. In Switzerland, for instance. I suppose the expense makes it impossible, but here we only seem able to keep the disease in check. There isn't much progress, you understand."

On seeing her mother, Eleni knew that quite the contrary was true. There had been progress, but on the part of the disease. Demeter was sitting by the window and had not risen. She reached out her hands, and the touch of those hands Eleni still remembered. They were as light and cold as snowflakes.

Eleni had echoed the priest's advice, and her mother had made the obvious reply. "Who would pay for such a thing?"

"The shop could be mortgaged."

"Your father wouldn't hear of that."

"I know he wouldn't."

"What's more," Demeter had said, "I wouldn't permit it."

"Mother, sometimes I can't help thinking that he just wants to keep you here, forever."

"That won't do, Eleni. You have no right to say such things. You don't understand."

"Please, Mother . . ."

"Don't interrupt me in the middle of a sentence, Eleni Lambros."

"I didn't interrupt you. . . ."

"And don't look at me that way." Demeter's voice was growing faint from exhaustion. Her face had remained stern as an aging Medusa's, a weapon in itself. Only the eyes were defenseless, deeply circled by such a beautiful and sad darkness that they inevitably overcame all emotions in Eleni except love.

"I'm sorry, Mother—to come here and argue with you."

"It isn't the arguing. It's what you feel. Eleni, if you have no love for your father, then how can you have any for me?"

"Mother, I want to love him. I do."

"You certainly don't sound it. Eleni, your father's the dearest man in the world to me. It's true he doesn't come here often, it's true that he's ashamed of me—my illness is like a weakness in himself. Your father is a very frightened man, but he does his best. And when he is most frightened and needs comfort, he comes to me. He came here after he put you on the plane. I had to hold his head in my lap. You look surprised. You think he is unfeeling, but with me, he can cry—a grown man. Now I think I've talked enough, and I want to hear all about Athens."

There had been several visits with her mother since then, and after each of them Eleni had gone with her basket of drugs and medicines to the woodside chapel in the hope of seeing Phaethon there, of having a chance to plead in behalf of Raphael. But Phaethon had not come, and now July was running out.

August arrived, hot and dry, and with it came a boat, sloshing so deep in the waves that she seemed more a vagrant wreck than a vessel propelled by a human crew. Eleni and Raphael were together on the beach and watched her burying her bow in every wave, lifting sluggishly above the sea ridges, her tattered sail like a bullet-riddled flag of surrender.

"She'll never make it," said Raphael. He had been lying prone on a high bank of pebbles, but now he sat with his knees drawn up, his head pillowed on his arms.

The dying craft wallowed onto the beach. A solitary figure leaped ashore. Eleni recognized him immediately from the high aristocratic forehead, the long black hair, the nervous grace. It was Jamal, and she ran to him.

"Allah be with you, Eleni," he said, his voice husky with relief, his impenetrable black eyes still wide from the hazards he had overcome.

"You shouldn't have come, Jamal! It's not safe for you." She knew very well that he had risked his life in doing so, and would risk it again if he stayed. She knew too that such courage was not natural to Jamal, but, like Phaethon's, was a controlled effort of will. Only in his aspirations toward the carefree life of a sailor was he like Raphael. "But thank you! Thank God you've come!"

"I heard about the *Nereid,* and then your letters. I owe Raphael a boat. If it hadn't been for me . . . well, anyway, here I am, Eleni. It's good to see you."

"And it's good to see you, Jamal." Warmly they clasped hands. She was grateful; the feeling suffused her like a blush.

"Where's Raphael?"

She had expected Raphael to run to Jamal as she had, but now she turned and saw him walking toward them with evident reluctance. They awaited him side by side, and if Raphael's manner were calculated to discourage, it had no apparent effect upon Jamal's enthusiasm.

There was no joy in Raphael's voice as he said, "You ought to have better sense, Jamal. Go home before you get yourself killed."

This reception of one whom Eleni was rapidly beginning to regard as a savior infuriated her. Still Jamal was eagerly smiling, holding out his hands with a loyalty no small slight could wither. "There's no use acting unfriendly," he said. "I'm here to stay. And I've brought you a present, down there."

"Generosity is the eighth deadly sin," said Raphael.

"All right, it's not a present, it's a debt. I owe you for one blown-up boat."

"Sail it back, Jamal."

"She'd sink. She needs some work. Take a look."

"Go back by bus, then," said Raphael. "I'm not getting you involved in this mess."

Jamal hesitated, seemed to take a deep breath. "Listen," he said, "there's an old Turkish proverb: 'Of the thirty-nine ways of avoiding danger, running away is best.' When the boat's fixed, we'll run away together. It's high time, Raphael."

"Don't you think it's a little late?"

"What's got into you?" demanded Jamal. "You're so full

of this *hahm-dah Lil-lah* nonsense you want to do absolutely nothing. Shake off your lethargy. A man in your position had better be energetic."

"All right, I'll put a message in a bottle and throw it into the sea. What do you expect me to do? I don't want my friends getting hurt."

Jamal turned to Eleni with a helpless shrug of his shoulders, but Eleni had been trying to move Raphael for two months with no success. She could not help now.

Once more Jamal took up the battle. "Raphael, that's defeatist talk, and you know it. I'm not going back to Larnaca. I'm a sailor, not a salt miner. I can't get this wreck going alone. I'm asking for your help."

"Now you're not playing fair." Raphael looked more stubborn than ever. He sat down on the damp sand and Jamal sat down beside him.

"All right," said Jamal, "we'll wait." Jamal had within him a coil of stoutest steel, usually hidden behind a mild exterior. Eleni became aware of it now and was grateful. For a while they sat in silence, then Jamal began to speak. He addressed neither Raphael nor Eleni, but rather spoke aloud to himself. "Now hearken to me, ye blessed ones of Allah, and hear of the wonders of the sea." His tone, the movement of his hands were those of an Arab bard. "When it's day and the sun's beating down, a fair ship is white sea foam scudding over the waves. And at night, with dolphins plunging alongside her bow, all glittery with fire, and her sails stretching overhead like silver, and not a sound on deck . . ."

Here Raphael interjected, "I'm shamed by your goodness."

But Jamal was wrapped in his narration. ". . . At night, a ship is like a wild sea bird . . ."

"I'm shamed by your goodness," repeated Raphael, standing up and offering Jamal his hand. "Let's have a look at her."

"She's worn out, as seaworthy as a water-soaked log," said Jamal.

The three walked together down to the shore, to the boat lying in the shallows with water almost up to its seats.

"Look at those lines . . . like dead snakes," said Raphael.

"You can poke your finger through the seams. Talk about the labors of Hercules . . ."

Beginning to laugh, they pointed out to each other the deficiencies of the old hull. She bore none of the loving touches of most caiques, no silver paint on the rusted cleats, no figurehead decked in gay colors, no blue and white barber-pole for a mast. In fact, there was scarcely any mast at all. Above a tin framed picture of Saint Catherine nailed about chest-high, the mast had broken off and been tentatively reset with wire and nails. "I thought we were finished when the mast came down," said Jamal, "but she's sturdy. She got here."

"She smells like a sponger," replied Raphael, and he was right. The foul milky slime of ten thousand perishing sponges permeated the planks.

"She's no prize, but look at that keel and those ribs. Any ordinary boat would have had a broken back by this time. She's a regular old dragon."

Raphael contradicted him with abrupt seriousness. "No, she's a lifeline, for you and me. She's the Ark." The air was charged with emotion. "You know the risk you're taking, Jamal."

"I know."

Thoughtfully and slowly they put out their hands to each other once again. Their fingers met and gripped hard. Both faces expressed the most joyous determination.

"I feel like running around the beach like a grinning dog," said Raphael.

"Let's not fritter away what's left of the day. Let's go to work."

With Eleni's help they bailed, and shoved the boat up above the tide. A lot of the planks would have to come out, even Eleni could see that, but the massive keel and the broad bow and beam of the ancient sponger were still a stout skeleton. Eleni worked with a will, and the world seemed to glitter like a spring day. Fervently she blessed Jamal, and his old hulk, which the three of them would turn into a sea bird, skimming far out to sea, safe from Cyprus.

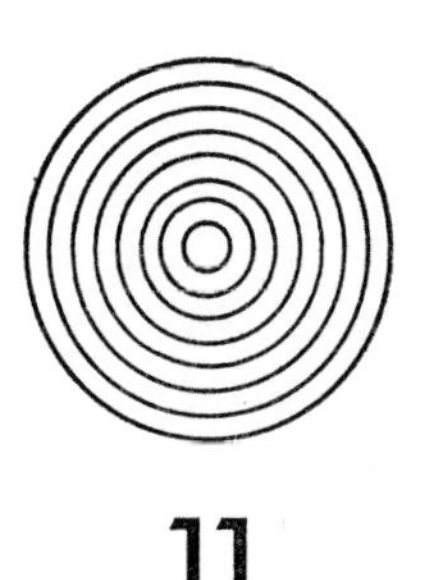

11

The "Wicked Days" of late August came with terrible heat. The molten sun did not rise from the sea, it overflowed. No rain fell on the parched earth. It stayed well out to sea in thunderheads that gave off a glow of heat lightning at night. Like the rain, the rebellion also withheld itself. Yet it was ever present in the air, like a noxious gas threatening all living things.

In many towns there were incidents. Eleni had only to switch on the radio to hear of killings and searches and masked men in the forests. The nights in Limassol and Nicosia were punctuated with the roar of grenades and the clang of police traffic. A Turkish police inspector was shot down in Xeros, his fiancée wounded. Some children found a cache of EOKA explosives in the crotch of an olive tree and all three were mutilated. But the EOKA offensive did not come. Some said it was because the caiques were not getting through with supplies. Others believed that Dighenis had been wounded. There were even rumors that he had gone mad. In any event, it was a summer of British successes. Commandos in support of Wren's Island police tracked down Markos Drakos, one of EOKA's chief lieutenants. Every time Eleni heard her father's radio, she expected news of Phaethon, of his capture or of his fiery death. There was no direct word of him, and though she continued to take drugs to the monastery, she did not see him. Nor did she want to see him, for now it was upon Jamal's boat, rather than Phaethon's good will, that she relied.

Most of the time she was out of touch with the terrorism. She was on the beach. Raphael and Jamal worked together with the rhythm of friends who work for themselves. Sometimes they sang, their untrained voices blending pleasantly. She did not intrude, though she worked too, with her face and body dripping sweat under the beating sun. She was good with a mallet, and drove the hand-wrought dowels so fast the mallet blurred in her hand like a fly's wing. The tip of her tongue protruded, from the effort. "Tomorrow," she told herself, "my hands'll be stiff as rigor mortis." They were much too stiff and blistered for oil painting, but that was of little importance. Soon she would only have to use a tar brush.

One evening as she was feeling sorry for her hands Raphael came, his feet dragging, his cross-cut saw hanging down like a whipped dog's tail.

"I feel as if all my muscles are tearing apart. They're separating from their anchoring bones."

"It's the sun that bothers me," she said. "Do I look like a red egg?"

"You shouldn't work as hard as you do, Eleni."

"I ought to work harder. How long will it take?" she asked. "It's almost autumn." Autumn was the deadline, as she well knew.

"As long as it has to," he told her.

"That may be too long."

"Don't look at it that way. We mustn't plan on things going well." Raphael spoke with a repose and conviction he had only just regained. Glancing along the beach at a group of half-naked English commandos, he added, "Besides, as long as they come down to swim, as long as you can hear their dogs barking, we're all right." Yes, Eleni felt good about the tracking dogs housed in barbed-wire enclosures behind the police barracks. As long as the dogs were here, Phaethon would not come. He had feared the dogs even when they existed only in his mind. "We're doing fine. Jamal'll have us launched in a week or two. I don't know how he keeps going. Look at him up there." Jamal was working on the old mast. The evening sun was behind him, setting his hair on fire with light. "Hey, Jamal! You look like a saint with a halo!" shouted Raphael.

"He is a saint," thought Eleni.

Jamal slid down the mast. He walked toward them with a gay resilient tread. "Well," he said, "if I am, I'm a weary one. Come on, you two, let's do some work." Good-naturedly he pulled the saw away from Raphael. It flopped over his shoulder and made a musical sound as he walked back to the boat.

"I'd better start sweating," said Raphael, "and you'd better go home. Almost curfew."

"I've hardly strength to make it," she said. "Well, I'll see you in the morning, bright and early. Take care, Raphael."

As she lay in bed that night, muscles all over her body kept contracting with weariness. "O sleep, it is a gentle thing," she began, reciting the old, half-forgotten school poem. "Beloved from pole to pole. To Mary Queen the praise be given. . . ." But it did not calm her limbs as it had done so often in the past. The quiet of the curfewed streets was broken only by the sound of dogs from behind the police barracks. Big, grave, sleepy-eyed brutes, they seemed to brood all day in some ancestral nightmare. With the cool of evening they awakened to bark until the sun and the heat returned. For weeks their ululations had kept Eleni awake, but she had learned the trick of following one isolated voice in the chorus; one voice, like a metronome, putting her to sleep.

The last week in August began with a surprise letter from Athens and an ugly conversation, neither of which Eleni would ever forget. The letter came first. It was from Uncle Andreas. Ecstatic with joy, he had sold one of her paintings. Money was enclosed, fresh drachma notes which came to ten Cypriot pounds. The buyer had been English and was coming back to examine the rest of her work. There was no telling what would come of this, the letter said; perhaps a scholarship to England. Overcome with euphoria, Eleni opened up her paint box. Some of the tubes had dried out already, and the brushes were impossibly caked. "Soon," she told herself, "soon." It took half a day of driving dowels in the hot sun to melt the excitement out of her body.

While labor stole her enthusiasm, an angry exchange with Father Grikos filled the gap with near despair. The priest had persuaded her father to build a hiding place under the fireplace for EOKA fugitives. Lazarus had agreed affably enough, but he complained to Eleni. "Blast him," he would say under his breath. "He's the most vicious priest who ever drew the breath of life. May God send a high wave to wash him from the world! If it weren't for your mother, I'd tell him to go to the devil." Eleni knew her father lacked the courage to face up to the priest under any circumstances. Lazarus was in the throes of one of these vain denunciations when Eleni told him, "Father, I think he's outside the door listening." Lazarus turned pale. "Perhaps if we open it," she continued, "he'll go away."

"We can't embarrass him. Give him time," said Lazarus.

"I'll go to the door and I'll call back to you that I'm going out," she whispered.

"All right. Go quickly."

She walked to the door and addressed it in a loud tone, "I'm going out, Father."

"Open it! Open it!" whispered Lazarus.

Eleni lifted the latch and swung the door wide. There stood Father Grikos smiling in the frame, as coolly as if he had been through this before and was not much surprised.

"Do I intrude?" he said, stepping inside. He began to talk amiably, complaining of a pack of English dogs that had escaped and run down the aisle of his chapel. One had lifted a leg at the iconostasis with such purpose that the priest's heart had nearly stopped. Since then, he had kept the chapel locked and his finished painting well above dog level. He went to the fireplace, inspected the hiding place, and approved the progress Lazarus had made. "We'll have need of that soon," he confided. "The great offensive is about to begin. I have told no one else." The statement was like the delivery of a precious gift which would leave Lazarus forever in his debt. "A caique is on the way—not far from here. It has to get through. With the arms aboard her and the ones to follow, we'll sweep the island of English . . . Turks along with them."

"Suppose the Turks fight back? I mean, the mainland Turks?" Eleni asked.

"So much the better. Do you imagine Greece will sit idly by in that case? Or our friends in America?"

"But what if the caique is taken? The others have been."

"With bare hands, then. There are more young Greek boys alive in Cyprus who will sacrifice themselves. They won't be put aside with talk, or the fact that without arms they cannot win. My dear, man is a fighting animal by nature."

"He's a domestic one!"

"A very womanly thought, my dear. But for a young man with spirit, it is better to live an hour as a lion than a lifetime as a lamb."

"Imagine how superior the lamb must feel after that first hour is over."

"There are worse ways for a boy to die," said the priest. He took a deep breath, his nostrils dilating on hairy depths. "A woman always has the personal view," he assured her. "You're thinking of Phaethon, of course. But set your mind at rest. He's a young man who won't be found wanting in a trial by fire."

"If you think he's a martyr, you're wrong," Eleni said. But about Phaethon she no longer felt sure. "It's so childish to want to die nobly for a cause. Can't you see it's better to live wisely for one?"

"Honestly, my dear, for a world to be saved, Christ had to be crucified," explained the priest. His voice was calm and agreeable, even though he was not used to being crossed.

"How can you compare a bunch of gunmen with Christ? Don't you see what I mean?"

"I see what you think you mean." His beady eyes were opaque, his smile dazzling in its insincerity. "Tell me the truth, Eleni. Has this change in your attitude anything to do with that excommunicated fisherman?"

"No, Father Grikos, it hasn't," she said, reddening.

"I hope it hasn't, because he's a marked man. It does your reputation no good to be seen constantly in his company."

Eleni stood quietly in what she intended to look like Christian resignation. Inwardly, she was boiling.

"I sense I'm not welcome here," said Father Grikos.

Lazarus looked up, startled. "Please, Father, sit down. I don't know what gets into Eleni. Eleni, you forget yourself!"

With an effort, she kept her voice level. "I'm sorry. I apologize."

"For what? I'm sure there was nothing personal in what you said. For myself, I try always to express God's will."

"Never your own?"

"God forbid that I should glory save in the Cross of Christ. On this earth I seek nothing for myself. Only Enosis for my people."

Eleni impulsively replied, "I hope your place in heaven isn't paid for by the rest of us."

"Eleni!" exclaimed Lazarus.

Father Grikos drummed his fingers on the table. "My dear girl, you're sorely mistaken if you think that. I've known your father for some time; I'm sure he can convince you of my motives as well as I can myself. At any rate, I haven't time for discussion. Lazarus, I'm leaving the chapel in your charge. The key's here on the table, should anyone need to get inside while I'm delivering my painting. And Eleni, while I'm gone, examine your conscience."

With this injunction, Father Grikos left them.

Lazarus slumped down in a chair, staring at the floor. Then he lifted his head and looked at Eleni with dead eyes. "Eleni, a girl of your intelligence, to say such things! Such stupid things! You couldn't have considered."

Close to tears, Eleni would not give in. As far as she was concerned, every word had been the truth. "Father, I can't help hating him. He uses you!"

"Like a cuspidor—I know," said Lazarus. "Eleni, this is the real world. A man must swallow a toad each morning to be sure of finding nothing more revolting on his plate before the day is over."

"I can't swallow a toad! I'd throw up. . . . Father, when I came home, I knew you'd have things for me to do. I told myself I'd do them so that nothing bad would happen to you or Mother. But this hiding place! I don't like what's happened already, and I'm afraid of what is going to happen. Can't we at least fill up the hiding place?"

"Eleni, I've lain awake nights. . . . I don't like it any more than you do, but if we're to give your mother the care she needs, what else can we do?"

"Do you imagine she's getting any better? She isn't. She needs specialists, a modern hospital." And Eleni went on to suggest he mortgage the shop. Lazarus was appalled, as she had known he would be, but what surprised her was the strength of his conviction.

"You haven't any idea how your mother and I feel about this shop—or about each other," he told her. "You couldn't have, because you weren't here in those early years. You don't know the sacrifices we made to get our shop going." He kept on, and on; his voice became for her the noise of an insect scraping its legs together. She was utterly dumfounded by his genuine belief, against the smashing evidence of his eyes, that he was helping Demeter. He thought that she was recovering. How could he? Was it because he could not afford to do otherwise?

"I've never been a brave man, like my brother."

"You don't know your brother," she interrupted. "You ought to visit him sometime."

"Don't despise me, Eleni."

"I despise what the priest is doing to you." Eleni, listening to her own words, immediately found unbearable a room filled with such a statement. She turned and rushed outside. The summer air was already too hot to breathe.

"Eleni, wait!" her father called after her retreating back. She stopped and said, "Yes, Father," haltingly, as though they were words just learned in a foreign tongue. Lazarus came up to her and put his hands on her shoulders. "Eleni, if you're going down to the beach again, I may be gone when you get back. I've an errand this evening in Limassol. A shipment of china ornaments."

"I know, Father. Those comic little black cats full of explosives."

"Yes . . . the cats. I'll leave the chapel key on the table. You know where to reach me if for any reason. . . . Here, Eleni, take my handkerchief. Wipe your nose." He offered his handkerchief, but she did not take it. She turned her back to him and walked down the street.

She worked harder than ever on the boat that day. The priest's threat, and the touch of September in the shadows, kept her going. Raphael and Jamal worked through without a break for lunch. They looked happy, so really happy that it lifted her spirits to watch them. They felt lucky, all three of them. Out of so many millions upon millions of years, for a few short days they were a triumphant trinity.

They scarcely spoke all day. There was no need for words; each had a task. It wasn't until late afternoon that Raphael stepped back and said, "Eleni, she's almost done. There's only the mast, and a little tar." He spoke with his eyes half closed in fabulous content. "If I could only make you understand what the sea means to me . . . but I've got to use words. You know, whenever I'm ashore too long, I feel as if I'm going mad. Listen, when she's all done, you'll learn to sail. We'll go to Africa, where the beaches are so hot you can bake bread without a fire, where the full moon dips so close to earth they say it's milked by the Pygmies. We'll be like Ulysses, except we won't make his mistake. We won't come home."

She didn't know whether he was serious or gently mocking.

"I meant to stay in Athens," she told him. "But I came home."

"And you're not sure you want to stay."

It infuriated her how well he read her thoughts. "Why do you say that?"

"You're a woman, descended from Eve. She found her garden too small. She wanted to leave. 'And go where, sweetheart?' asked Adam. 'Outside.' 'But there's hard work and sickness and death out there.' . . . well, you know the rest." Raphael gave a great, involuntary yawn which flowered into a laugh as he tried to smother it. "In a few days it will be goodbye to Cyprus."

"Will you go far?"

"We'll go as far as we have to."

"I want you to go, but I can't imagine Cyprus without you."

"Then come along. You'll have to come along," he urged.

"Even if you were serious, I couldn't. Not now, not with Mother the way she is. And Father. . . . Raphael, you've got to go right away. Don't come back until this mess is over." She had not the slightest doubt that if he delayed he would be killed, and the thought of life without him was like suddenly going blind.

"Don't worry," he said. "I have a personal sort of god who looks after me. I have luck."

"You mean you've got Jamal. Luck isn't a god."

"It's the only one when your God and Allah are subtracted from one another. But don't worry, I don't put much faith in luck either."

"Then go away before Father Grikos gets back, before Phaethon has a chance to do something."

"Have you seen Phaethon, Eleni?"

"Not lately. Why?"

"Would you fly into his arms, if you did?"

She laughed aloud. "What a silly question! Raphael, what do you know about flying?" Clearly he was embarrassed. She became more serious. "I'm afraid he may do you some great harm. I feel it. And I used to think I understood him. . . ."

"Each of us, like the moon, has a dark side, Eleni."

"It seems to be the only side he has left," she said sadly.

On the beach the late sunlight streamed through the rusty loops and canopies of drying nets. The air bore a dreamlike quality, as if a shower of mica dust had come from the sun. The sea itself was a pane of frosted glass; far out, the shuddering of heat lightning passed again and again through the clouds.

"Eleni, you'll never marry him. I can't imagine it. There's a saying, 'Happy is the man who, before dying, has the good fortune to sail the Aegean.' It doesn't have to be a man, Eleni. What if you really were to come with us?" She was listening now in astonishment. "Eleni, it's not easy to plead one's own cause. They say a man who falls in love with a mermaid loses the power of speech."

"Don't play-act," she told him.

"I'm not play-acting." He spoke with a fury in which she detected a note of the histrionic. "We could sail down to Limassol and be married there. Jamal would be the best man, and I know two musicians, one with a saz and one with a mandolin."

"Marriage is a serious thing," was all she could manage in reply.

"I'm trying to be as serious as I know how." His solemn voice sank to the heart of their relationship.

Around them night was falling, hazy and purple. Vague green and blue luminescences persisted behind the old Venetian castle while the cloudy sea blazed with color.

"I ought to be scared," she thought. "I ought to have lots

of reservations." But for the moment she could find none.

"Raphael, where would we live? Up the beach on a pile of sand?"

"A home's a thing that people build between them," he told her. "Besides, there's the new *Nereid.*"

"I can't imagine . . . the two of us sailing away . . ." The thought so outstripped her emotions that she actually managed to sound calm.

"Well, the three of us. Only a couple of days, and she'll be ready."

Slowly she held up her wrists as if they were joined by handcuffs before dropping them back into her lap.

"Why the handcuffs?" he asked.

"I told you. My parents. Somehow I've got to get Mother into a good sanitarium."

"All right, we'll dive for treasure. We'll find a statue of Aphrodite and sell it to a museum. . . . What more can you do here?"

She didn't answer but said instead, "When all this mess is over, we'll talk about it, Raphael."

"You mean when life's over?" If this was a barb, she ignored it. "I'm not very good at being impatient, Eleni."

"What sort of a name would I have? I don't even know your last name."

"You'd be Mrs. Raphael, I guess," he said, laughing. "I don't know. I really don't know who or what I am. My father was Maltese, but not by blood. My mother, Greek and Italian. A dash of Moroccan and Turkish, too. I'm swarming with nationalities."

"I don't mind that."

"What about living on a boat?"

"I'll get seasick."

"Then I'll cut a lemon and hold it to your nose."

"Eating octopus makes me sick, too."

"Not once you're used to the taste of the sea."

"All right, I'll get used to it. I'll have to take my paints along. Will you mind my paints?"

"I'll love your paints. Oh, Eleni, we'll have a time! We'll hoist our red sail any time we please and head for the open sea. What a sail! Like blood! Wait till you see it! We won't be bothered by anybody except the gulls. No money, no luggage, no Mondays or Saturdays, just the warm sun on the clean deck, sailing to the horizon."

Eleni was silent. She liked to hear the fisherman talk of his love for the sea, but when he spoke of racing white clouds she thought of storms; when he described the scudding waves she imagined the terrifying depths below them. After a while he grew silent, too. Slowly the dusk encircled them. Far off, the incandescent flashes of lightning clawed at the mountains of Turkey like a battle of dragons. In the cove the wind was rising, sending waves thumping on the beach.

Jamal had stopped work and was watching them from the boat. When Eleni waved he called out, "Do you know it's getting late?" Joining them, he added, "Whenever this time of day comes round, I feel like one of Hercules' children." They didn't understand, and he explained, "Didn't he mistake them for salamanders in the dark, and eat all six? I don't want EOKA making that kind of mistake with us, even if you do. Help me build up the fire." Obediently Raphael followed him, but over the sound of the wind, over the roar of the waves, Eleni heard the voices of dogs. She remembered the curfew and knew she would have to hurry home. As she went reluctantly up the beach, she glanced back to see the first glow of their fire. With its light they could work far into the night, but she could not help thinking that unlike Hercules' brood, they would be safer in the dark.

Eleni passed through a thousand cool shadows where the cicadas were screaming. She was afraid of autumn's coming. Toward the village, a dog complained of his confinement. His voice became a chorus, and almost unwillingly Eleni felt herself drawn in the direction of the wire enclosures. Watching the feeding of the dogs, their training in what was called "the assault against man," had become a favorite evening pastime in New Paphos. A crowd had gathered at a safe distance from where the dogs stood with their forelegs pressed wide against the wire mesh and their heads thrown back.

While she watched, a man clad from head to foot in a thick padding of canvas and cork emerged from the barracks. He strode awkwardly along the fence like a knight in armor, while the dogs leaped in terrible fury. They seemed about to gnash through the steel with their teeth to get at him. The mummy wrapped in asbestos entered an empty enclosure. A British sergeant entered behind him with the leashed dogs and the gate was locked. With brisk commands, the sergeant put the dogs through their drill like obedient puppets. Their gleaming eyes seemed to contain no more life than their bodies, but rather a cold and impersonal malignance. Then the mummy, who had been propped against the far wall, waddled into the dusty center of the kennel. Behind him, the sergeant loosed the first dog and gave a sharp command. The animal flung itself upon the mummy, who did not see the attack coming. Gropingly he tried to free himself, but the creature was upon him, its teeth fixed in the cork headpiece. The man could only struggle like a diver moving deep beneath the sea.

No wonder Phaethon did not come, thought Eleni. In a kind of trance she watched the scene, which seemed brought forward by a trick of time from some primeval jungle. The effect was enhanced by the ruddy light of evening and the swirling dust. The sergeant had released the second dog, and finally a third. Under their attack, the victim was immobilized, his unsteady legs farther and farther apart until he fell flat, a man upon an operating table. The dogs covered him.

Strange to think of these dogs as her protectors, but they would keep Phaethon and his agents away for a time. Every day more dogs were arriving on the island. Cyprus was becoming a dog kennel. Or was it a kennel for men?

From a nearby street there came a sound. She told herself it was a motorcycle backfiring, but it could as easily have been a pistol shot.

She hurried home to an empty house, the voices of the dogs howling behind her.

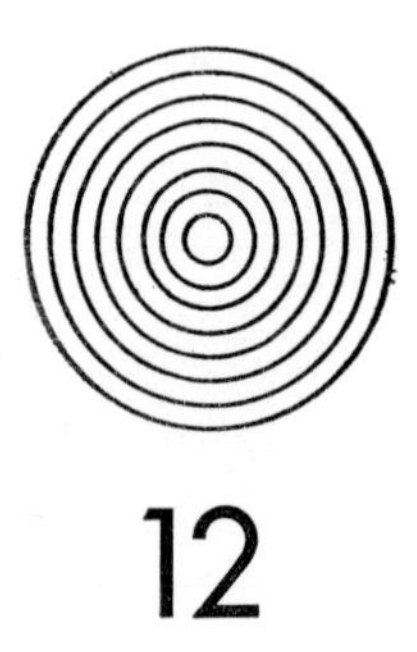

12

Eleni did not sleep well that night. The house itself did not seem to sleep. The framework creaked and stirred along with the plaintive chorus of dogs moaning in the darkness. A series of barks, a long wail, then silence. Eleni would find herself bracing for the next outburst as the man in the cork suit must tense for the attack. "Can't they be quiet for a change?" she said aloud, and then realized slowly, at first with disbelief, that there was no sound in the night.

Finally she entered a shallow sleep of unrefreshing dreams in which she tossed all night. "Phaethon, don't do it, please!" She was with him in the forest and he was striking matches and throwing them about. The dream was so real that she seemed to smell the smoke.

Although she had slept badly, she woke early with a feeling of disaster. Her first thought, possibly because of the dream, was that the house was on fire. She heard it crackling and leaped from bed only to laugh at herself. It was the sound of silkworms gnawing at the mulberry leaves. Still, the smoke was real enough, and there was something wrong with the dawn. It had a prehistoric look, dull and yellow and brooding over the land.

"Oh God!" she said. "Forest fire . . . a big one." With trembling fingers she dressed herself in the gloom, then ran outside. Other people lingered in the road, gazing toward the Troodos Mountains, where a wrathful sun rose behind coppery shreds of smoke.

To calm her nerves, Eleni opened the shop early. A few customers came and confirmed her fears that the fire had begun in Cedar Valley, not far from Chrysorroyiatissa Monastery. Later, when a truck appeared in the street calling for volunteers over a loudspeaker, she knew the fire was out of control. Cedar Valley was a long way from the monastery, but the smoke was already in Paphos, over the sea. Up there it must be pouring into her mother's ruined lungs.

Eleni decided to telephone her father in Limassol. There he might be able to hire a cab and bring Demeter back home. Once she was safe with her family, they would no longer be dependent on EOKA. They could make plans for a sanatorium in Europe. With this thought in mind, she picked up the shop telephone. She seldom used the mysterious little instrument. "Hello," she said into its cold black ear. She placed the trunk call with the operator, and after a long series of clicks, heard the disembodied voice of her father speaking from thirty-five miles away.

"Lambros here."

"Father, it's me—Eleni."

"Lambros here." To whatever she said, he repeated the phrase in a sort of infuriating paroxysm.

"Father, can't you hear me? . . . Father!"

"Lambros here"—one last time, and the line hummed in Eleni's ear.

Completely discouraged, she replaced the receiver in its hook as though it weighed a ton.

Of course she could go alone, but bringing her mother safely home would not be an easy task. She thought of Father Grikos. He had a cart and a mule, and he had influence, but she had seen him depart with his savage painting the day before. She could not depend on finding him at the monastery. There was the army and the St. John's ambulance services, yet they would never carry Demeter home but to some other shelter among strangers. That was no answer; Eleni wanted her mother home. Of course she could rely on Raphael to help, but she was reluctant to delay his departure. The alternatives were clear and simple enough, she told herself, but no answers came. Instinctively she moved toward the beach. As she passed the kennels, she saw that they were empty. That explained the abrupt silence in the night. It might well explain the fire.

She ran the last part of the way and arrived with a hand pressed against her throat. "Oh, I'm not used to running so fast!" Jamal, who had been tarring the hull, looked up. "He's down inside," he said, but at the sound of voices Raphael had emerged on deck, so tall and strong she could have wept.

"Here for the launching? We've only got to hang paper lanterns," he said gaily, and vaulted over the side of the boat onto the sand. "Hey, what's the matter?"

In that instant, she had decided not to ask Raphael. She had no right to involve him.

"I just came down to see the *Nereid*."

"Oh, no, you don't. I have only to look at you. What is it? Tell me everything and I shall understand—everything."

So she told him about her mother. She did not ask him to come.

"You'll want me to go along," he said.

"I don't. I don't at all." She spoke emphatically, too emphatically.

"Eleni, you have such wonderful trust in your eyes. I'll be ready in three minutes."

"It's too dangerous for you."

"EOKA? I'm not worried about them with the army swarming all over."

"Still, you ought to sail. Jamal shouldn't sit here waiting, especially with the dogs gone."

Raphael and Jamal conferred. The boat was seaworthy and only the rigging had to be finished. Jamal promised to do that, with the boat anchored far out.

"Don't worry about me," he told Eleni.

"Come on, let's get started," said Raphael. When she continued to protest, he added, "All right, you go and I'll follow. It'll look silly, but that seems to be the way you want it."

Eleni made no further objections, but said suddenly, passionately, "Raphael, you're so good! You too, Jamal. Both of you . . ."

"Jamal's the saint. When I do something, it's out of pure selfishness, believe me."

"Even so, I have a feeling you'd never let me down, no matter what." And this expression of trust came to the fisherman like a command he could never disobey.

There remained only a few last words with Jamal. "We'll be back tomorrow—day after, at the latest," Raphael told him. By then the boat would be launched and decorated and ready for the sea.

"Goodbye, Jamal, and thank you." Eleni made an effort to put warmth and gratitude into the commonplace words, for she knew she was placing a burden on Jamal as well as Raphael. She was asking the two of them to play at being Hercules' children for another dangerous night.

"Go with the good," Jamal called after them as Eleni and Raphael left the beach. The sky above the distant mountains was a dusky yellow from spent flames.

They went the entire way on foot. No buses were running toward the Troodos, but there were convoys of other vehicles. British three-tonners and brilliant yellow tractors moved in the direction of the smoke, which rose ever higher like the eruption of a new volcano. Twenty thousand feet above the sea it hung, over Gordon Highlanders, Marine commandos, Greek and Turkish volunteers from Skouriotissa and Lefka villages. There were young women among the volunteers, tough and boisterous as the men, with mattocks and rakes in their hands and black scarves over their heads. Trucks full of British and Cypriot fire fighters ground up the roads to Troodos, raising clouds of dust to mingle with the smoke.

Because of the dust, it was impossible for Eleni and Raphael to walk close to the road. They made their way through the tobacco-colored fields, past the old threshing floors. Some farmers kept on winnowing their wheat, but others had left their jobs to fight the fire. During the blistering midday hours, Eleni and Raphael rested under the shade of a giant carob. Here sheep were pastured, but few of them moved in the heat. A pair of lambs gamboled in the vibrant sunlight and a half-naked shepherd boy romped with them.

"How can he?" said Eleni. Her lips were crusted with dust.

"Because he isn't real," said Raphael. "His ears are furry and pointed, and if you rolled up his pants, you'd see hoofs."

"I don't need cheering up," she said.
"You look as if you do."
"Well, it's not supposed to show."
"If you're hot now, just think how it must be up there," and he jerked his head in the direction of the mountains.

When they finally reached the monastery, it was no longer hot. Evening and a rising north wind had brought with them a winter chill.

Since Eleni had last seen the place, it had changed into a fire camp with cooks, camp crews, tool sharpeners, truck drivers, not to mention fire rakes, mauls, double-bitten axes. Contemplation seemed irreparably shattered by an atmosphere of frantic confusion. Eleni looked about for Father Grikos's cart but could not find it. Then Father Constantine came toward them, sails spread, full of the cargo of his woes.

"Oh, my poor trees!" he cried.

"Have you seen Father Grikos?" she asked him.

"He was here yesterday with that fiendish painting. That devil behind the Cross! May he swim in God's blood. . . ." These words he uttered with the earnestness of a prayer. His voice was infantile with weariness, and his face reminded Eleni of a lopsided balloon which age has begun to pucker.

She did not question him further about Father Grikos, and a phone call from the fire station at Kykko called him away.

With Raphael she found her way to Demeter's room. Her mother sat in deep shadow, the room lit by a solitary candle. She looked brittle, her face moving toward deeper wrinkles. The windows were closed because of the smoke, and mechanically she stirred the air with a heavy black fan.

The fan stopped and she looked up.

"Eleni, what are you doing here? Is that Raphael with

you?" Her disease, and the trial by smoke inhalation, had left their mark, but her vitality still held. "I hate to scold you, but really! To come here at such a time."

"It's too unhealthy for you, Mother. We've come to take you home."

"Home? How romantic you are, Eleni. You see danger in a little smoke. It will rain by tomorrow morning. The wireless says so. . . . Come here. I can scarcely see you way over there. Come here, Raphael. Let's have a look at you, too."

Nothing more was said about Eleni's plan to take Demeter home. Nothing needed to be said, for she was determined beyond persuasion. One way or another, she was taking her mother home and from there to a proper hospital, no matter how far it might be.

They talked for a while of old times, and despite her protestations it was quite obvious that Demeter welcomed their arrival. She coughed frequently and held a handkerchief to her mouth. It was not the white handkerchief she used to carry, but one with flowers painted on it. Roses.

Eleni touched her mother's forehead. It was like a lamp that had burned all night.

"Now why did you do that?" the sick woman demanded.

"You've a fever, Mother."

"What do you know of such things, Eleni? I'm perfectly all right."

"You ought to be in bed, Mother."

"I'll get sleep enough later on."

"Well, we've had a long day, Raphael and I. We're tired."

They went to the door. Before they closed it, Demeter snuffed out the candle as if an expression had crossed her face which she did not wish them to see. From the dark corridor they could hear her cough.

"She's thin as a winter wren," said Raphael. "I had no idea . . ."

Outside, fire fighters were being fed. They ate squatting, straddling logs, stretched out at full length. A few wandered slowly up and down as they chewed, like peripatetic philosophers.

"I'll get us some food," said Raphael.

"I don't want any," she told him. "I haven't the strength to chew."

"Don't be silly, Eleni." He brought her a tin platter of meat and bread. The meat was dark and only slightly cooked, with skeletal fingers of fat showing through it. But the bread was fresh. In her hunger, it seemed to Eleni to have a Biblical goodness.

"Well," he said, "hungry after all. I like the way you eat. Most women pick at their food."

With the cessation of hunger came greater weariness. Eleni felt her legs dying under her. The fire fighters lay about on the ground like men shot down in battle.

There wasn't blood in her veins any more, there was lead, and except for the cold, she would have slept instantly. The wind and the cold seemed worse than the fire itself, which glowed an angry pink in the distance.

Her misery must have shown, for Raphael said, "Don't let things get you down. Try to sleep . . . rest, anyway. Think about the stars."

Between the tall pines the sky was milky with them. The pines swayed with the rising breeze; their needles were washed pure silver in the starlight and the eddying smoke from the campfires. The distant flames seemed to lick the stars.

"Look, a shooting star!"

"I don't know about God or Allah," said Raphael, "but when I see a star fall through space, I believe in something. I wouldn't call it God. . . . You know, during the day when you're out in a boat and the sky is solid blue, it's like a wall protecting you from what's behind."

"What is behind?" she asked.

"Nothing but the stars, I suppose. The night."

The stars were retreating now, their rays faint, almost obscured by the smoke. Their augury was dark and stern, Eleni thought. Then gradually the shadowy smoke began to thin, the stars and the lanterns in the camp shone brighter and brighter.

"If I pray, I'll be able to sleep," she said.

"Long ago, prayers were the daughters of Zeus, and they were wrinkled sad creatures who made it their business to follow sin about."

"What prayers do you use?"

"None," he said regretfully, then added, "Once in a while, when I'm lonely, I pray for a good boat and a quiet sea."

This wasn't conversation, thought Eleni. It was thinking aloud.

"Are you going to pray for rain?" Raphael asked her.

"It's worked before."

"Well, go ahead, Eleni. But afterward, try to rest."

So she prayed that the rain would come and help the men stifle the flames. She prayed for her mother's recovery and for peace in Cyprus. Before she was finished, she noticed that Raphael was asleep, lying very solemnly on his back with his fingers entwined across his chest. Because of the thickening smoke, he breathed hissingly through his teeth. She prayed that he would return safely to his boat and that Jamal would be protected on his lonely vigil. She prayed finally for herself, that she might live long enough to be a great artist, like El Greco, who had come from Crete. These were the extravagant prayers of half sleep, and her eyelids had closed in honest repose when something broke the peace. It was like wind; rushing, distant, terrible.

Eleni sat up. She was about to conclude it was a figment of her semi-consciousness when she heard it again, a slow breath rippling over the mountainsides, rousing an unearthly emotion. Some of the fire fighters sat up. "Rain!" someone shouted. Then it arrived at the monastery; not rain, but the north wind with all its force. It sighed through the black foliage, bending down the trees. Out on the black horizon, the distant flames seemed to stand higher, brighter, and nearer.

Her fears received prompt confirmation with the growling arrivel of Land-Rovers. They belonged to the R.A.F. mountain rescue unit. Loudly they cursed the Cypriot volunteers for panicking in the gusts of wind. If they hadn't deserted the fire line it might have held, according to the soldiers, but now the fire was out of control. Presently men arrived on foot, like soldiers of old, with axes and mattocks. Blackened with ash, dirty, sullen, exhausted, they cursed the English in turn. To Eleni, they seemed near mutiny. But the thought of special pay held them—the pay and their exhaustion. They weren't ready to face the task of going home that night. They were beaten.

Last of all came the students from the forestry college at Prodhromos. Their clothes were torn and filthy; their eyes were red with fatigue and smoke irritation. They looked much like the other Cypriotes, but they did not swear aloud and they followed thc directions of one man—rangy, tall, but folded upon his tallness. Eleni recognized him by his size and his piratical mustache. Phaethon had often described the headmaster during his time of study at the school.

She went up to him. "What do you want? News from the inferno?" His abrupt tone made it very evident that he did not wish to talk. When she identified him correctly, he seemed surprised. "I don't know you, do I? If it's one of the boys you're worried about, they're all here . . . safe . . . for the time being."

That wasn't what she had intended to ask, but it was all she got, directly. The man sat down, stretched out his legs, and groaned. It seemed tactless to question him further, but she did not leave. There was talk among the students, and Eleni listened intently as the details came out. They had worked on the fire line for a day and a night until the villagers had panicked when a wave of wind hit. All the flaming snags had flared up like burning flags. The fire had jumped the line and within twenty seconds there wasn't any line left.

"If the fools had only stuck it out," said the headmaster. Apparently a rumor had been spread that the British helicopters flying overhead and dropping food parcels were actually dropping bombs. Then at the critical moment a priest had turned up on the fire line, or a terrorist masquerading as a priest, damning all those who dared obstruct God's flaming path. That had precipitated the panic. There wasn't any use complaining now. The fire had broken loose in the dark and was pouring over the forest in a flood. For seven miles it advanced on an unbroken front. "Not while any of us are alive will that forest be the same again."

"What will we do now?" asked one of the students.

"Try to rest," the headmaster told him.

"I mean about the fire."

"Build another line. A mile or so from here."

"That near?"

"There isn't any other place we stand a chance."

"Does anyone know how it started?" interjected Eleni.

"Most fires come from lightning."

"Not this one," interrupted one of the students.

"No," said the headmaster. "This one started in three places at the same time, or as close to the same time as it would take a man to run from one place to the other."

"Damn the EOKA anyway," said the student. "This revolution goes on too long. It's a bore."

"You think the fire was set?" asked Eleni.

"We *know* it was set. It has to be that fellow who left school. You'd have to know something about forests to destroy one so completely."

"He was an odd one," said the headmaster. "When you bit on that Phaethon, your teeth always seemed to hit bone."

"Phaethon!" Eleni's voice was barely audible.

"Odd name, isn't it?" replied the headmaster. "He was the reckless sort of young fellow who'd finish everything off—put a torpedo under the Ark if he had a chance."

"May his bones sweat pitch," said the student.

Eleni never questioned them, never doubted in her mind that Phaethon was the one. How could he do such a thing! His heart must have completely leaked out, leaving him little more than a cracked shell.

It was a cold and exhausted sleep to which she returned. After what seemed only moments of unconsciousness, she was awakened by such a strange cry that she was afraid to sleep again.

She sat up, coughing. The monastery grounds seemed drenched in swirling moonlight. She recognized it as the sun. Barely visible in the smoke, a hawk floated on motionless wings. Its cry was weird and restless. Then the smoke concealed it entirely.

"Good morning. You slept late," said Raphael. "What's on your mind? You look like a wistful sphinx."

"We can't stay here any longer," she said. "I want to get Mother home."

"There's no easy way to get home. How far can your mother walk, anyway?"

"Her legs aren't sick."

"Eleni, she's an invalid. Her chances are better here."

"Here? She's dying here. The fire's only killing her that much quicker."

Eleni's mind had all along been made up. If there was any chance of saving her mother, of freeing her father from EOKA coercion, the first step was getting her mother home. Practical difficulties no longer mattered.

Raphael picked a piece of grass and sucked it thoughtfully. Finally he said, "It's about five miles, mostly downhill, to Dhimitrianos. That'd be like Calvary to a woman in your mother's condition."

"She can walk, part way. I can help her, I'll carry her. Forget about us. I didn't ask you. Go back to your boat!" She was being unfair and she knew it. But the last days had brought her to the brink of hysteria.

"Hush, Eleni, we're going. We're going, so calm down, and we'll try to figure out the best way." According to Raphael, three roads led down from the monastery. Two wandered farther into the mountains before turning toward the coast. The third was blocked by fire. This left as the only possible choice a short cut toward which the fire was rapidly progressing. "With fire it's always a gamble," he said, his dark sweet eyes full of a sort of bravado. "Who knows? They say the skies up here are crawling with saints. Can we count on a miracle?"

Eleni had relied on his support, but she expected resistance from her mother. There was very little. Demeter was willing and submissive. She closed her eyes when she spoke, and her voice came weak and serene. "I know what's wrong with me."

"We'll be home tomorrow, Mother," Eleni tried to divert her.

"I'm nothing but breath, and not much of that. I'll need a great deal of help." Demeter's words fell from her lips like crumbs of dry cake.

Eleni looked around for some cloths, dampened them, and made Demeter hold them to her mouth and nose.

"Ready?" Raphael put his arm beneath Demeter's shoulder and gently assisted the sick woman down the corridor and out into the mysterious daylight. An invisible sun moved somewhere behind impenetrable screens of drifting smoke.

The fire fighters had gone. The place seemed deserted except for two monks, one of whom walked fatly while the other rode a small donkey. His sharp knees were raised so that his feet would not touch the ground. They were arguing, and Eleni recognized Father Constantine at once by his voice. When they drew nearer, she realized the monk on the donkey was Father Grikos. Fear and hatred made her hesitate; then she ran to the priest, concern for Demeter overcoming all other emotion.

His black cassock was scorched brown by fire, smeared gray with ash, but for someone who appeared to have been singed by hell's brimstone, Father Grikos's response to the girl's plea was kindly. Then Demeter and Raphael arrived. Raphael tried to pass by unnoticed, but Father Grikos urged his donkey up against him. Veins wriggled in the priest's forehead and one hand was raised, the fingers partly closed as though about the shaft of a thunderbolt.

"Execrated of God!" he shouted. "Leave this sanctuary!" He pulled the little donkey aside to let Raphael pass, but blocked the way again before Eleni and Demeter could follow. "I have warned you repeatedly, Eleni!" he admonished. "But you, Demeter! Beware association with the godless!"

"May Grikos beware of Grikos," replied Demeter quietly.

"Come," he commanded, "we will go find my wagon." But Demeter had taken a step from the path. She passed him by, and Eleni went with her. "Stop! It is a terrible sin to ignore God's voice!" But they did not look back. Eleni could hear Father Constantine's voice raised in vain protest, but she could not distinguish his words. Grikos drowned him out. "Be accursed, then! Be accursed into everlasting fire!"

There was nothing but smoke, flames, and the deep forest ahead of them.

The priests were already veiled by smoke when Eleni and Demeter came to where Raphael was waiting.

"I heard Father Grikos," he said. "I think you should accept his offer of the cart."

"I have never liked that man," said Demeter. "My family will not be beholden to him, not any more." Eleni and Raphael looked at one another. Both knew Demeter's disease-ridden body had not weakened her stubborn will. To argue would be to waste words. Raphael took her arm, saying, "As long as we keep the wind to our right side, we won't get lost." Where the path turned away, they left it for the fields and headed toward the first fringe of forest. Here the trees were old. Here wild animals passed unnoticed; hedgehogs, hares, and foxes fled from the common danger, running to safety, or panicked and ran to the fire, which would indifferently engulf them.

Early in their trek, Eleni, Demeter, and Raphael passed close behind the new fire line, which hooked gradually away to the north. Two days without rest and little food had made the fire fighters slow and fretful. Eleni heard a voice raised briefly in an old Greek song, "Forty years a bandit chief . . ." Cyprus had no songs of its own. The voice broke off in coughing as wisps of smoke drifted across the line. Ashes and bits of blackened bark were already falling.

What Eleni knew of fire fighting, she had learned from Phaethon. She knew that a fire had to be starved to death, imprisoned within a strip of nonflammable earth. First the strip, miles long in this case, must be cleared, and then a backfire lit to widen the safety band. But a backfire was a tricky weapon. If lit too soon and driven by the prevailing wind, it could become as fierce and as menacing as the fire it was designed to destroy. A proper backfire must be lit at the moment the prevailing wind had died and began to give way to the opposite draft from the forest fire. Even here there was danger; sparks, panic, any number of possibilities on a seven-mile front.

Eleni could no longer see the fire fighters, though their voices were close at hand. She could hardly see the trees, for they were lit neither by the sun nor the moon, and what illumination there was, was dying.

The gusts of wind were becoming more erratic. It didn't seem possible that the fire could be so close. Yet the silence of the forest was no silence but a steady roar like a surf to which one has become accustomed.

"What's happened to the wind?" said Eleni. She felt her chest too small for her heart. She was lost, they all were lost. Inside her mouth, the saliva was glutinous and bitter.

"Come on! Follow me," called Raphael.

So far, Demeter had stayed on her feet, leaning on Raphael's arm and making frequent stops. Now he picked her up gently. A muffled protest came from behind the cloth that Demeter pressed constantly to her mouth and nose, but Raphael ignored it. "You're light as a leaf," he assured her. Then he called to Eleni, "Hurry!"

Eleni followed close behind his lunging bulk. In spite of his burden, his groping feet never seemed to stumble or hesitate. Somewhere in this eye-watering, lung-burning fog, she knew a thin line of terrified, smoke-grimed men were waiting. A few experienced ones, like caricatures of Olympic runners, trotted along that line with sparkling fuses. Every few yards they would touch the blue-white torches to the duff and needles, setting the backfire upon which everything depended.

In that instant the whole woodland seemed to pause in

unearthly apprehension. Hundreds of humans and forest creatures were waiting, listening, as the fires approached one another. One such creature was a mouflon, a wild ram that had fled from the fire for two days. He stood now at bay between the onrushing flames, eyes blinded, horns lowered. A lesser creature might have sunk to its knees in ritual sacrifice. The mouflon with its last strength charged the backfire, burst through in flames, and ran straight on across the line of men and cleared soil and into the forest. He ran wildly through the trees for another two hundred yards, a figure of terrible loneliness.

Eleni saw the mouflon coming, dimly at first, as a great ball of orange-tipped feathers that staggered as it went and finally fell. Along its meteoric path, flames sprang up.

Trained fire fighters would have quickly smothered this overflow, but when volunteers saw flames behind them, some withdrew cautiously, tools in hand, and others panicked and burst into the forest, scattering their implements. Up and down the line, confusion spread.

Eleni heard the rumble of flames to the north, the steady roar of an express train. Men came bounding like wide-eyed deer, and with them the first red snowstorm of sparks. Terror-stricken, she stood with her hands pressed against the sides of her head.

Raphael stumbled toward her. "Get back!" he shouted. "To that stony ridge. . . . Hurry! Hold on to my belt."

The danger had robbed her of judgment; she had enough sense left to know that, and to recognize that Raphael was one of those rare individuals who seem strengthened in mind and body by impending disaster.

He had already started off when she told her arms, her legs what to do. In her terror, she advised all parts of herself to follow Raphael.

The sparks of the meeting fires, thrown high and carried

far over the unguarded line, became gradually a solid wall of flame, with long-reaching arms and isolated spot fires. With great leaps and bounds the men ran away from it, but the sparks sailed along ahead of them, and only the experienced ones looked for burned-out patches in which to throw themselves face-down.

Behind her and to one side, Eleni heard the cruel thunder of the fire crowning in the pines. Not just a single tree, but often as much as an acre of superheated woodland would explode in an instant.

Following Raphael, she was not at first conscious of a change in terrain. The trees had thinned and here and there ridges of rock broke the soil.

"This way! This way!" Raphael dragged her to a place among rocks where a trickling stream moistened the ground. "My God, what luck!" he exclaimed. He placed Demeter on the ground and began to smear her dress with mud from the spring. She never moved, but she kept the rags tight against her face.

"Put mud on yourself," he commanded. Dumbly Eleni did as she was told. The mud was thick as molasses and dripped back into the tiny pool with a slow flob, flob.

"Face down now!" he shouted.

All three lay flat, and Eleni felt his arm around her, a shield from the primeval storm. Overhead the flames sounded like thunder, but across them rushed a cool draft. There was no real heat in it yet.

Eleni looked through a thickening rain of sparks like fiery beads, and she could see Raphael's mouth shape words. "Nothing is going to happen to us," he said. For a long moment, fear was lost in his nearness. "I'm a sailor. I wasn't born to burn up in a place like this."

"Hold my hand tight," she said. Her own hand, despite the growing heat, was deathly cold.

"Listen, whenever the smoke clears, breathe. There'll be pockets of air. Don't breathe the smoke. It'll be hot from now on."

The crown fire and the ground fire advanced in unison, the one burning through the underbrush, heating the trees above, the other throwing sparks ahead. It was almost upon them. The heat enveloped them.

Right under her nose, tiny black ants moved faster and faster on their mysterious errands. Even they could feel the heat. It would shrivel them up. It would shrivel everything up, and but for Raphael's arm about her, Eleni would have bolted. For her this wasn't a fire any more, it was the angel of death raging overhead. Wildly she began to pray. "Oh, Mother of God, get me out of here. Dear sweet Mother of God, please, please!" Something crashed against the back of her head and she saw a large burning pine cone roll away. Her head hurt so much it was hard to think about God. She found herself counting as though each number were a prayer. "Three, four, oh Holy Mother! Six, seven . . . this heat! Please! Oh, God!" Her lungs were searing and the world was swirling away in little red pieces. Behind her eyes she seemed to see terrible creatures of fire, goatish beings, all flaming. Hither and thither, they slid about her, entwining their fiery arms and tails.

Eleni had no doubt they would all die. But even as this grim presentiment came to her, the fire was changing. On the level ridge of broken stone, it was losing vigor. The soil was thin and rocky and the few pines were stunted and thinly scattered. Only beyond the ridge, where the ground fell away into thick forest, could the crown fire renew itself.

No longer did she feel the weight of Raphael's arm around her, and the air that entered her lungs seemed cool. Eleni turned, looked up into the smoky air through which the afternoon sun grinned down like a mouthful of flames. Then she noticed Raphael. She thought at first he was doing a comical victory dance until she realized he was slapping at widening holes that blossomed like red roses in his shirt and trousers. She sprang to her feet, her hands full of mud and water from the spring. Together they put the fires out, but not before his legs, shoulders, and hands were covered with yellow blisters. Like small jellyfish, they seemed to cling to his skin.

"Oh, Raphael, your poor hands!" She wanted to touch each terrible blister with the healing touch of Christ, but she did not even have butter to soothe his burns. "How do you feel?"

"I don't know," he replied evenly. "Right now, I don't hurt."

Her throat choked up and her eyes felt foolish with tears. "We didn't die, Raphael. We didn't die . . ." She embraced him with a sort of anguish, and all at once he began to tremble.

"Don't fuss over me. Look after your mother."

"Mother!" She had forgotten Demeter.

Demeter had not stirred. She looked dead. Her face was gray, that part of it which Eleni could see. Eleni knelt beside her, heard a struggling, half-strangled breath. She took away the sooty cloth, washed it, and gave it back to her mother, who never complained of pain. She was beyond speech and clung silently to Eleni like an exhausted child.

Far down the ridge the fire moved away, throwing up a towering column of smoke, charred needles, and bark. It had spared them, but were they much better off? A burned boy, a lost girl, and a helpless woman, abandoned in a desolated wilderness where not so much as a fly was stirring. Eleni felt despair overwhelming her once again. "Christ and the Madonna have mercy on us," she said under her breath. Then Raphael was beside her, bending over Demeter. "Raphael, your burns . . ."

"I'm like a fish. . . . I don't feel pain," he told her, but his voice was low and husky, as if all the weariness in his body had risen into his throat to call him liar. His face frightened her. It looked as if he were holding his will and his body together with a valiant smile.

"Mother's got to rest. There's no use trying to move her tonight."

When Raphael spoke, it was to Demeter. "I want to tell you something. You're a lady—a real one. I'll have a doctor here before midnight. That's a promise." He stood up straight, seemed to brace himself. "I'm all right, Eleni. I'll be back." Before she could decide whether to protest or not, he had turned and was moving off into the ruined forest. Except for the tall snags of dead trees, the wind had blown the fire out, but she did not like to think what would happen to his feet if his shoes were burned through by the still-smoldering ground.

She lost him among the snags, saw him once again, then finally lost him entirely. She and her mother were alone in the late afternoon of a day that seemed so long she must have been a child when it began.

Demeter was filled with pain. It left very little room for thoughts or speech, but she managed one last, gasping gallantry. "Don't look at me as though I'm dying. It's only the growing pains of old age." She breathed as though she had just been dragged up half-drowned from a well. "Eleni . . ."

"Don't talk, Mother. Rest."

"We owe that boy our lives, Eleni."

"Hush now." Eleni held her hand to her mother's lips. "Hush."

Demeter said no more. It took all the strength of her indomitable will to keep on breathing.

Yes, Eleni thought, she had seen their lives saved. She had seen them saved, and she felt confident, as though through some actual pact with fate, that Raphael would return soon with help and save her mother a second time. How strange that the beach vagabond of her childhood, a loner whose happiness thrived in solitude and on the sea, should become so involved with the lives of others. Her life would always be involved with his. She knew it, beyond the shadow of any doubt. Whatever she might once have thought, whatever others said of him, she loved him, for all his mad dreaming. Perhaps she loved him because of it, for his dreaming was more beautiful than the reality of other men. What was more, he seemed to have the gift of life. Others like herself might stand back, hide, put life on canvas, but in Raphael she sensed a passionate happiness, bound up with his boat and his independence. These were his essential truths, and for a time she had stolen them from him. She would give them back now. She would make him take them back.

The September night was coming down and with it Eleni felt the chill of a glacial wind. She tried to protect her mother with her own body. What had become of Raphael? She imagined him lost, fallen among smoldering embers. All she could see in the thickening night were hundreds of glowing spots like cats' eyes where the fire lurked. Above the winking forest, a half-eaten moon looked down.

"If Raphael doesn't come back, I've got to think what to do." She could leave her mother and look for help, or she could try to take Demeter along. Her head felt large and hollow and echoing, incapable of any decision. Her tongue was so round and dry that it stuck to her lips. She drank from the spring and would have moistened Demeter's lips as well, had she not been asleep. She seemed to hear the long drawn-out note of a bugle. Hope returned, but the note went on and on, longer than a man could hold his breath. The imagined sound came from her head. Silence surrounded her. There was not even the whir of a cicada.

Eleni was half conscious from fatigue when Raphael touched her on the shoulder.

"You're back!"

They kissed in the ancient way, joyfully, on both cheeks, and for a moment it was as though they had fallen in love from sheer relief.

With Raphael were two men: one, a little wiry grasshopper of a man; the other, thick of trunk, with an air of comic purposefulness. Both were British soldiers, and Raphael introduced them. The dead handshake Eleni exchanged with both was an honest expression of their mutual fatigue.

"There's an ambulance waiting, with patients. We've got to hurry," one of the soldiers explained.

The stretcher went first. Demeter lay on it with one foot hanging over the edge, her head flat on the pillow. Eleni walked close beside her. A north wind probed through her clothing, numbing the pain in her tired muscles. She was so cold she had to clench her teeth to stop shivering, but exultation filled her at the miracle of their rescue.

"Most of the time I must have been lost," said Raphael. "Then I stumbled onto a road. My shoes were going to pieces, so I was lucky to find it. An ambulance came along only a few minutes ago. . . . Look, you can see the red blinker light."

"I don't know how you ever found us."

"I guess because I had to."

The ambulance smelled of antiseptic and the sweet stench of damaged bodies. A doctor with fierce bushy eyebrows and a stubbly chin stood in the road, chewing gum. The stock figure seemed familiar to Eleni.

"All right," he said, "let's have a look at this one."

He examined Demeter with a flashlight.

"Inside, next to the girl," he told the stretcher bearers. "The other two in back as well."

Eleni and Raphael crouched in the ambulance. Along with the doctor, and Demeter, there were two patients, both badly burned. One was an English soldier who seemed to be in dreadful pain. He groaned rhythmically, with the sound of an old man dying. The other was a girl, deeply and unhealthily asleep. Her dry cracked mouth was open, and she shuddered continuously.

"That's frightful," whispered Eleni, who wanted with all her heart to help. But parched as she was from the fire, she could not even manage a sympathetic tear.

"What is?" asked the doctor.

"A child, hurt like that."

"Both her parents were lost. That forest is no place to bring up children. But don't worry. She won't ever know what happened to them. She won't ever feel the pain, she's too badly hurt. . . . Look here, don't I know you?" He held the flashlight to Eleni's face. "Yes, the girl from the bus accident. That boy'll pull through, thanks to you. . . . Well, I thought you'd like to know." Eleni nodded. "This is your mother, then? Let's have another look at her."

"She's tubercular," said Eleni.

The doctor examined Demeter more carefully. He chewed a great wad of gum and rasped his unshaven chin with his thumb from time to time. "Well," he said finally, "as far as I can tell, the fire didn't hurt her on the outside. Not a mark that won't wash off. Inside, though . . . without an X ray, I wouldn't want to say, but I'd guess her lungs are burning up. Not much left of them. There simply aren't the right facilities on this island. . . . Why hasn't she been sent to a decent clinic?"

"Money," whispered Eleni.

"Yes, it always comes down to that," said the doctor. "At

least I can give her a shot for the pain. I don't suppose you have access to oxygen? You know, the kind bottled under pressure. Look here, I'll give you a note. . . . You can take it round to whoever's in charge in the Paphos district. This ought to fetch you some oxygen and a medical orderly to go with it."

The burned soldier seemed to be conscious again. He called for morphia with a very young, very English accent. "Morphi-ah . . ."

"Hang on, old boy," said the doctor. "We're nearly there."

"Morphi-ah," mouthed the lips.

"He isn't really feeling it yet," said the doctor sadly. "By tomorrow he'll just be pain covered with skin . . . and not much skin."

"Will he die too?" asked Eleni.

"I don't think so. They'll fly him out of here tomorrow. A good hospital, a year or so of skin grafting—he'll be as good as new."

Eleni peered ahead where the lights picked up the mountain road. She thought of Phaethon. He had set the fire and caused the pain and death. Could she ever feel anything but hatred for such a person? She thought also of money, of more than a lifetime of saving to provide for her mother. There was great weariness in her eyes, but also great determination.

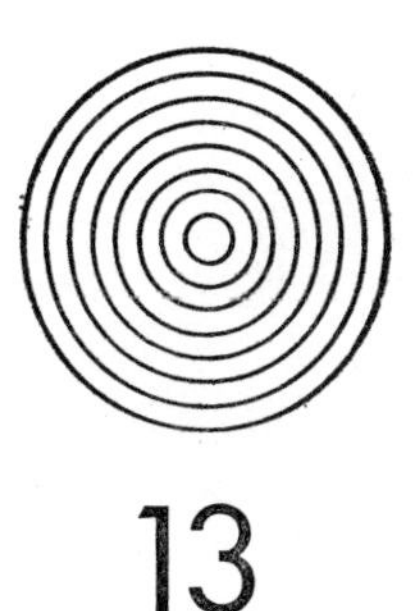

13

Eleni walked on the beach at Paphos. Behind her rose towering clouds of smoke, but she did not see them. She walked toward the sea and waded out until the water was above her waist. There she paused to moisten her hands and wrists against the shock of the water. Then she dove. The bubbles of her descent frothed past her ears as she swam into the colder layers, but she scarcely felt the chill against her sun-warmed skin. Rising to the surface, she stroked steadily toward a blue-black line where clouds built up and drove with the early evening wind toward Cyprus.

Eleni swam strongly. She would keep on swimming as long as there was strength in her limbs. Then it would come to an end—all the emptiness and all the guilt.

It was a late summer sea into which she swam, full of creeping cold currents. Fish brushed against her feet. She could see them far down in the clear depths. The brilliant water was full of life, life in which she had renounced all part. Everything had been left behind. Her friendships with Phaethon and Jamal and Raphael were finished. Her duties to her parents and to Cyprus were fulfilled. The things she had loved, the need to paint, the desire even to think were lost in the slow motion of her arms and legs. Still the memory was there, not as deliberate thoughts but as pictures imbedded behind her eyes, terrible pictures of a night and a dawn and a morning that seemed to have irreparably smashed her world.

Once again Eleni saw the ambulance drawn up to the house. She saw herself banging on the echoing door.

Her father had appeared with a smoky lamp that threw a coppery light, deepening the creases between his eyebrows and throwing wrinkles into his nasal folds. Demeter's face on the pillow was like a casting of faded bronze. Lazarus slumped before her stretcher as though before a wailing wall. From his lips came the ancient lament, "Aiee, Aiee," but softly, as though he dared not disturb his wife.

"At last he knows," Eleni had told herself. "At last he understands." The terrible night seemed to be ending well, with the three people she most loved safely together. Then the first intruder emerged from the house and leaned over her mother. "Demeter, my dear!" said Father Grikos in an unctuous tone, as though their recent exchange were expunged from the record. "They have done you good! Look at the color in those cheeks!" His words sounded like some fearful misquotation from a popular song. To Eleni he whispered, "Your mother will never stand erect again. God will have her soon." From this moment on, she hated Grikos with an implacable hatred. His God was a great enemy. He never failed to intrude, to steal.

Near the shore the water was emerald green, but where she swam now it was black, shot through with arrows of light to interminable depths. It was colder, too, with a Black Sea wave of melted ice. She tried to think only about the waves and the sea, but the memory pictures had started again.

They had carried Demeter inside, her father at the head of the stretcher, Raphael with his burned hands and herself straining at the foot. Inside the front room they set Demeter down. Eleni leaned panting against the wall. Only at the priest's loud summons, "Come up! Come up from there, both of you!" had Eleni noticed that the stone base of the fireplace had been removed. As she watched, a form wriggled up from the hole beneath. Like a genii from a bottle, Phaethon emerged.

His eyes roved the room, peering like those of a child in a strange attic. "Ah, Eleni!" he said. "Raphael, too. . . . I heard dogs barking."

Eleni sensed another crisis and it made her weak. She was too tired to listen to the ravings of a pyromaniac, and she feared the possible consequences for Raphael.

"There aren't any dogs," Father Grikos said. "Join us."

"A howling dog means death," Phaethon insisted in the still of the September night.

Gun in hand, smelling of sweat and fire, another form rose through the secret door like a boar at bay.

"Ah, my old comrade-in-arms!" exclaimed the priest. His cavernous nostrils dilated with excitement, and he added with a thrill of inspiration, "You come from God! Verily, verily, this is the encampment and the army of the knights of God!"

In the trembling lamp light, Eleni recognized the new arrival. It was Dighenis, the Leader, and the ground seemed to fall away beneath her feet. Ignoring the priest's rhetoric, Dighenis stood on the balls of his feet as if about to spring, but his gaze was anchored on the infinite. In a last attempt, his voice fading, Father Grikos intoned, "Honor to those who guard their Thermopylae. . . ."

"They are digging up from below," the Leader mumbled. "They are trying to get at me from below. . . ." He paced along the whitewashed wall, and where his fingers pressed, the whitewash flecked away.

Eleni had been completely dumfounded at first, but a dispute between Phaethon and the priest brought some clarification. Father Grikos wanted to press on to the ancient burying vault where munitions were stored. "The weapons will give us all new life!" he shouted. "We will drive the Turks from the island. Yea, weeping may endure for the night, but victory cometh in the morning!"

Phaethon was adamant. Until the Leader regained his composure, they would stay in the hiding place. For a moment the pair seemed magnetized, chin to chin, but it was Phaethon who dominated.

Grikos gave up grudgingly. "Then purify him, Lord, and let him lead."

"I do hear dogs!" Phaethon exclaimed.

"Dogs," echoed the Leader, a mindless refrain. Eleni knew what had roused the pack. They were barking at the coming of dawn.

The tearing open of a door stopped the dispute and riveted all eyes on Lazarus, standing blackly in the frame. Behind him the day was breaking and the voices of the dogs were loud. As unemotionally as one might comment on the weather, he told them to find another hiding place. Eleni heard the priest's faint snort of surprise as her father said, "Damn you, get out of my house!" His voice was not loud, but it vibrated with fury long suppressed.

Phaethon had snatched the dangling gun from Dighenis. It was not much of a weapon, but its splayed muzzle was wide enough to hold a wine cork. "Go ahead, shoot," Lazarus told him. "The army'll be down on you before you can reach the door."

"You'll regret this, Lazarus, until the day you die," Father Grikos cried. Her father did not reply. With his right hand, he made an obscene and final gesture toward the door. Trembling, Father Grikos leaned toward him and whispered, "What God protects you? Allah? Is it Allah?" He shook his fist until his whole body quivered.

All this Eleni seemed to see for the second time more clearly than the vivid sea about her. Her arms continued to stroke mechanically. The sea lifted her and a distant sail at the same time. She saw it rocking over the horizon. It came into her view from time to time and then was lost. Once more she beheld only the small smoky room full of angry men.

Demeter lay on the stretcher, gray and motionless, her eyes tightly closed. Phaethon turned upon Raphael. "If we can't stay here, we need your boat." His tone was threatening, as if he expected resistance.

"Are you planning to sail away?" Raphael asked, almost cordially.

"We've no choice," Phaethon told him. The old rifle with its single chamber was crooked in his arm. Eleni expected a protest, but Raphael answered, "I didn't say you couldn't borrow her. You can." Eleni was shocked and overjoyed at the same time. She hoped the two old friends would shake hands, and they did. Grinning self-consciously, Phaethon stuck out his hand and Raphael jerked his out to meet it. There still seemed to be a fondness between them.

Phaethon said, "I wouldn't have done anything with the gun. I mean it. I was only pulling your leg."

"It nearly came off."

Phaethon turned. "Those dogs! Are they still barking from the kennels?"

"They're in the streets," Raphael told him. He offered to guide them by the safest route to the shore.

"All right, hurry! Lead us!"

"Pontius Pilate! God will not let you wash your hands of this. . . . I'll see to that!" shrieked Father Grikos at his former host.

"You are a coward! Though you be ordained in God's own tears, you are a coward!"

"For the love of God, Lazarus!"

"Yes, for the love of God . . ."

She had not seen her father since, but she no longer feared for him. He had found his courage. She no longer feared for her mother's health. She had taken care of that—and now she would pay the price for it, for everything. Through the cold dark water, her limbs looked green, already dead. She gulped a mouthful of spray, spat it out, struck out with her right arm, then with her left. She was still strong, but there would come a moment of weariness when her mouth would open involuntarily and she would draw into herself the silence and the coldness of the sea. This seemed the answer to all self-accusation.

"This way, this way!" Raphael had cried, and guided them down the dawn street where dust ghosts whirled in a breeze from the sea. Phaethon followed close behind, his manner stealthy as one with nothing to lose and perhaps something to gain. In his right hand, held away from his body as though to fight off interference, was the old gun. His left hand, a sort of rudder, rested on the shoulder of his leader.

"The dogs are louder! They're coming this way!"

Raphael led them toward the Turkish quarter, with its carved screen windows and large doors, all bolted. "Keep going!" Phaethon ordered. The dogs grew constantly louder, and he prodded Eleni with the muzzle of the gun. They began to run. Dighenis moved awkardly, like a man in his sleep. Wordless sounds issued from his confused dark soul, the sounds of a baffled quarry. Father Grikos lurched along, his gown held up and his skinny white legs pumping.

"If you and your father have betrayed us," Phaethon threatened, "by God I'll . . ." He grabbed her by the wrist and pulled her along. Eleni did not struggle, and with the others she was impelled into the fields that bordered the Turkish dwellings. Here the vines were high, and Phaethon pushed her down into them. The scent of earth and grapes rose in her nostrils. She expected to die here. Irrationally she thought of Hector, perishing before the walls of Troy, whose last thoughts had been of the sweet smell of the soil.

Father Grikos had fallen beside her. He lay on his back, with his waxen nose a deathly yellow in the faint dawn light. His dry lips moved. "Pray for us sinners now and at the hour of our death. Pray for us sinners . . ." She felt better, knowing he was terrified.

The patrol had already reached the street of the Turks. The white eye of a flashlight winked as though conveying a message in code. Phaethon clamped his hand over Eleni's mouth. The fingers of his other hand dug painfully into the flesh of her shoulder. But the flashlight left the fields, its glow balanced by the dawn. It bobbed down the street. The baying of dogs changed to a single savage note. A pistol shot . . . snarls . . . triumphant barks. "It's someone else. They're after someone else! And they're tearing him to pieces!" Phaethon whispered.

"Thank God!" the priest exclaimed.

A Sten gun chattered.

"Praise God for victory! Praise God for victory!" the priest's voice still soared, but he carried none of them with him.

"I'm sorry, Eleni," Phaethon said, "I should have known better. I should have trusted you. It's just that our leader's life is so vital. Without him our cause is lost!" Led by that madman, they were forever lost—Eleni hadn't the slightest doubt of it.

"He'll never lead you," she told Phaethon. "You have only to look at his eyes. He has no mind left. He won't lead you or anyone else again."

"Not with his mind, but with his body. Do you know men who are not afraid of God are afraid of him? As long as he lives and I'm with him, I can be his mind. That's why I have to be so . . . well, ruthless for the cause."

"All three of us have the same aim. A great and sacred one," interjected Father Grikos.

"If you want to know," Phaethon said, "he's the mad one. You should have seen him roaring through the forest with a torch in his hand. My God! He's a regular priest of fire, that Grikos. If you had the chance, you'd burn this island to a cinder, wouldn't you, Grikos?" The last words were full of contempt, a contempt that did not seem to register in the Scriptural reply. "If in truth, ye anoint me king over you, then come and put your trust in my shadow; and if not, let fire come out of the bramble, and devour the cedars of Lebanon!"

"You hear that? King over us!"

"Judges 9:15," said the priest.

"You didn't set the fire?" Eleni asked Phaethon.

"How could I? Oh, I know I talked about it. But that's my forest. I loved that forest. . . . Come on, let's get to the beach."

This revelation had been for Eleni a ray of light illuminating Phaethon's somber spirit. It had seemed as dazzling as the light which shot down about her now, throwing her shadow deep beneath the waves. There was a fable that a drowned person's shadow watches for him in the water, and deep down, her own shadow twinkled and glided as though it were alive and breathing there. But it was only an empty shadow, she knew, even as the revelation of goodness in Phaethon had turned out to lack all substance.

Phaethon had hurried them toward the beach. The bright dawn was retreating behind thunderheads that stood out to sea. The clouds were so huge the small caique seemed a toy beneath them. It rested with its prow upon the sand, its sail furled and its deck empty. A bowline led into the shallows, and the sea hissed against it as though it were red hot. Jamal walked down the beach and Phaethon intercepted him, directing them all to the *Nereid.* They went one after another over the stern and down into the small cabin, which contained two bunks set in the hull, a blackened iron stove raised from the old *Nereid*, a plaster statuette of King Edward the Seventh bought by Raphael's grandfather in a distant port. The six of them filled it. They remained standing except for Jamal, who sat with his knees drawn up, eyes fixed straight ahead.

Raphael had turned quietly to him. "My friend," he explained, "I had to lead them here. They would have come without me in any case, but they don't need you. Go home."

The young Turk's brow was set and he made no reply.

"He doesn't go. We need a crew," Phaethon told them.

In the distance the barking of dogs resounded, hard on another scent.

Despite the menace in Phaethon's voice, Raphael walked to the stern. Jamal rose and followed him. Together they went over the side into the water. Phaethon, who had already begun tugging at the anchor line, demanded to know what they were doing.

"Pushing you off," Raphael told him, and they shoved the boat free of the beach.

"Get aboard! Hurry!" shouted Phaethon.

"I said you could take the *Nereid,*" Raphael told him, "but we're staying in Cyprus."

"We're not sailors, and you know it!"

"We won't report you. Come on, Eleni." Raphael held out his hand.

But Eleni shook her head and silently prayed that Raphael would understand. She was convinced that any attempt on her part to cross Phaethon now would bring disaster on them all.

Father Grikos opened his mouth in an outpouring of damnation, a shrill echo of his days of power. As if in response rose the voices of dogs. To their howls the Leader seemed to listen, jaw slack, face blank, as though awakening to the sounds of a jungle. In a moment that called for decisive action, he made no move. Only his fingers responded, writhing at his sides like the pale tentacles of a squid caught in a net.

"Someone has set those dogs after us," said Phaethon, glaring down at Raphael.

"I've been with you the whole time," the fisherman replied. Against all logic, Phaethon seemed determined to accuse his old friend.

"Don't be afraid. No harm will come to any of you through me," Raphael assured him.

Phaethon's reply was deadly. "Get back and rig this boat or I'll kill you!" The pitch of his voice rose sharply.

Eleni expected an act of equal fury, but Phaethon wavered, turning instinctively to Dighenis. The leader replied not a word. Like the ship's looming figurehead, he stood stiffly at the bow. Only his fingers were alive and slowly writhing.

"Shoot him!" Father Grikos screeched.

With a great sob, Phaethon vaulted into the water. He did not aim the gun, but held it overhead as a club. Eleni shouted a warning, and Raphael turned to meet the attack at the water's edge.

Phaethon circled, a predatory beast around a dangerous prey.

"Raphael," he shouted, "for God's sake, come back! Do as I say!"

Raphael awaited him, looking down at his great brownish hands as though in surprise. Normally they were clubs that could fell a man, but now they were so blistered from the fire he could scarcely make them into fists.

Phaethon lunged, bringing down the rifle. Raphael caught it in midflight, twisted it, and shoved his assailant into the water. As Phaethon struggled to rise, Jamal approached, and in the young Turk's hands was a nail-riven shaft of driftwood. Raphael waved this assistance aside and received Phaethon's cruel blow to the body without giving an inch. Once more, Eleni saw Phaethon shoved back into the sea.

Raphael gained the sand. He followed Jamal along the rim of the cove while Phaethon thrashed in the water searching for his gun. He did not find it, but floundered ashore with a rock in his hands. It was like their childhood fights, and Eleni felt the blood in her head sucked down by a vacuum in her chest.

"Raphael!" she screamed.

This time Raphael did not turn. Jamal did, but he turned too late. Phaethon delivered a sledging blow. Once and again the stone descended, and like a toppling tower splashed with red Jamal fell, his feet still on the shore, his chest, his face in the water.

For Eleni, the world became a confusion of electricity. There were small explosions of light in the air and inside her head. She heard her own voice screaming, thin and high like a gull's voice. She saw Raphael run to where his comrade lay. She saw the others, that unholy trinity, disappear along the beach.

All this she had seen and still saw inside her head as she swam, stroking hard as though she might outswim the memory. And she would. Eventually the sea would wash her clean.

The cold was in Eleni's arms and legs. The current rather than her own efforts carried her, no longer out to sea but along the coast. Under the last opal glow of afternoon, the beaches of Cyprus glided by. Was this Aphrodite's beach already? Had the current carried her that far? How long had it been since Raphael knelt in the sand at Paphos?

Small waves had lapped against his knees. He had not moved from them, but crouched forward in pain and elemental suffering. Through repetition, his incoherent words resolved themselves into "Allah! Allah!" over and over again, the voice rising and falling.

Then the beach rang with another sound. It was the urgent protest of dogs addressed to the walls of the Frankish castle, to the carob trees swaying in the breeze, and to the shore, where the three fugitives had disappeared. Back and forth along the water's edge the pack ran, their voices shrill in defeat.

She knew that Jamal was dead and that Phaethon had escaped to a cave full of explosives. She saw the English soldiers pouring onto the beach after their dogs. She sat in the anchored boat as though it were another world. There she remained hypnotized, aware of events yet unfeeling, as though her heart and mind required some future event to release the dammed-up torrent of her emotions.

An English officer approached her, asking questions in a voice that came to her ears from a great distance, from a world in which for a moment she had no interest. "Miss, you saw what happened here. A boy's been killed. Would you recognize the man who did it?" She did not answer. "There were three of them, weren't there? Did you see where they went?" Still she did not speak, even in denial. "Let the bloody beaches pile up with poor wretched Turks. Just pieces of garbage. You know the English'll come round with their trucks and clean up the mess before it brings the flies. That's right, isn't it, miss? Don't you even mind the flies? Nothing to say? I didn't think so. . . . Sergeant, hang on to this girl . . ."

As if in the middle of a nightmare Eleni watched the officer depart, saw the dogs barking helplessly at the sea. The nightmare would go on, interminably repeating itself. Seldom came a chance to awaken and break the cycle. These people, if they could stand by uselessly while a child lay broken in the street, could as readily watch their island gasp out its life. Seldom came a time to interrupt the dream sequence, but in this passing moment she had that opportunity. It might never come again in her lifetime. Reluctantly she started after the officer, a sleepwalker at first on uncertain feet. By the time she had caught up, her steps were sure. Eleni had always tried to live by the simple rules. Thou shalt not kill. Thou shalt do unto others. . . . But there were times when these simple rules no longer applied to particular cases. "This way, I'll lead you," she told the English captain. She could not look at him. She could not look back at the troop of armed men that followed her down the beach and into the fields, which were pitted with ancient tombs. Behind her, held in check by their trainers, the dogs crept forward like an insidious fire.

"There." Incredibly, her own voice spoke again. "You will find them there. Everything, in there." And the soldiers moved forward toward the tomb where Phaethon used to hide as a child from his father. A voice shouted through an electric megaphone and it was answered by shots.

"Get down here, miss." The captain pulled her out of the line of fire. "I suppose what you're looking for is the reward, but you've done a fine thing for Cyprus. Maybe now there'll be peace for a while."

"Reward?" Eleni began to shiver.

"Ten thousand pounds if we finish off Dighenis. . . . I think we will."

"I don't want money," she said, as much to herself as to the soldier. "I didn't do it for the reward." She assured herself that this was true, although she had always heard about the bounty.

"Everyone can use money, miss."

A voice which she could scarcely believe was her own replied, "Is it enough to send a sick woman to a hospital in Europe?"

"And more, I should say. A great deal more," came the reply.

The money . . . for her mother's sake she could not refuse it.

Nearby a machine gun opened fire, and with each shattering burst her eyes blinked. She could not control them, and when the captain asked her to go home, she started off on hands and knees. When the cave was out of sight, she rose to her feet, walking slowly at first, then faster, until she was running toward the sea with her fists clenched.

When she came to a broken wall overlooking the bay, she leaned against it. Before her stretched the sea, its serene surface mottled with sunshine and shadow, its horizon piling up with ominous clouds. Then she saw it, already far out: a tiny sail puffed by the wind. The *Nereid* was heading toward the storm.

She walked slowly across the beach, entering the shed where Jamal and Raphael had slept during the last weeks. Here Raphael must have borne the body of his friend, but there remained no trace. Aimlessly she searched for associations which might bring them back, but they had left little behind. They were simply a chunk of her life fallen into the sea, down deep below the deepest prisms in the blue-green water.

Outside the shed, she sat in the sand. These last hours had become a narrow bend in a pipe through which she was unable to force her emotions. Impersonally her brain recorded the facts. Jamal was dead. Phaethon soon would die. Raphael had sailed away and she would not see him again. These convictions changed the whole structure of her life as though the keystone of an arch had been stolen. She alone was to blame. Her letter had brought Jamal here. Even so, death had waited patiently for her to intervene between itself and Jamal. She had been given every opportunity to save him, but she had failed, and failing, had lost Raphael as well. And Phaethon? However humane her motives, she had ordered his execution.

All day Eleni stayed there. She heard intermittent shots in the distance, so faint they were not real, and the bells of a flock of sheep. Toward late afternoon the migrant vultures began rising from the fields on the updrafts. Their wings sounded across the water like the beating of fans.

The larger world paid no attention to her tragedy. It paid no tribute to those who had died, and when she herself was dead, the world would go on with its bright sunlight and its dark storms. The fate of a human being was no more than a drop, however sparkling, in an infinite sea.

With the first hint of evening the gri-gris boats began circling with lowered nets. The old fishermen with their crab-apple faces and tobacco-stained mustaches worked them carefully with the knowledge of generations. The circle drew tighter on the invisible net as she watched, and she heard the fishermen uttering hoarse cries and beating the water with their oars. The water in the closing eye of the circle became thick, like a meat stew which is coming to a boil. The fish swarmed and darted, trapped in the dripping nets, and were hauled aboard shimmering like spilt coins.

The hour before sunset had come. Fleecy red clouds had gathered which looked like ships one moment and cranes the next. Suddenly the event which she had half expected took place. A violent explosion, a flash, and then a cloud ripped the island's horizon. Like a divine translation from Ezekiel, the great mass of smoke and debris rose billowing up and out. A concussion followed, with the hiss of trees bent down before the blast. The impact rushed across the beach like the legendary sound of ancient gods deserting a doomed city.

There followed a funereal hush. No rifles broke the calm. No dogs barked. The fishermen stood motionless in their boats while the cloud rolled upward toward the sunset, then began to fade and merge from the working of the wind.

Serenity returned. The sunset began. The fishermen returned to their toil. She could no longer be sure that it had not taken place a thousand years ago. Everything seemed rooted in the past as though etched forever on a brazen shield, with one generation after another acting out the consequences of those etchings. The only hope seemed to lie in taking no part in the flow of things, to draw no sword, to vanish. That had been Raphael's solution.

Strange how her short life was at once so full of happenings and yet so empty. There seemed nothing about it that she wanted to save. She took one last look at the beach, at the fishermen and their gilded nets, at the shed where the young fishermen had lived. Then she stepped into the sea.

Silently now the clouds drifted above her and silently the sea tangle drifted far below. The gray air was still before the storm. Whether it was the swimming or the sight of the blue and distant beaches, Eleni experienced a gradual lifting of her spirits. How beautiful it all seemed, how strangely desirable in this last glimpse. She remembered her last sight of the Acropolis. How lovely it had been, though how changed from her expectations.

Over Cyprus night was falling, hazy and purple. The pealing of a chapel bell carried across the water, and occasionally the fragrance of grass. Out at sea the storm gathered, its blackness shattered again and again by lightning. Her last view of the world was to be a lovely one, and she was amazed at her own awareness of the beauty around her. With the darkness and the storm there would be only the counting of her heartbeats, and finally the arrival of the moment when she must open her mouth to the salt water. This would not have been Raphael's answer. She knew that. To Raphael the sea was a place of baptism and rebirth. He would never surrender his life willingly, not even if she lay dead on the beach. "It's not good to mourn," he had said to her once. "You'll be dead yourself before you can bring anyone back to life." No, Raphael would never have chosen to swim to the end of his strength. She had little time left now. She awaited the end uncritically, made no motion toward the beach. If only there had been time for one last painting, she might have tried the shield of Achilles as she had so often imagined it. At the bottom of her final abdication, there remained this small "yes" to life. It seemed almost sufficient to rebuild everything. To paint and never get involved, to live on the beach as Raphael had done. Even then, one could not be sure. Raphael would escape in his boat, but wherever she might flee there would be her burden of guilt. There seemed no other way. Whatever she did, she could not avoid a place on the shield of Achilles. No one could, not even Raphael. She seemed to see Father Grikos's painting before her, a final triumph of stupidity in the world. He was there in the painting, torch in hand, the priest of fire and destruction, and beside him was Dighenis, the insane leader whom warriors followed. And there was Phaethon—he wore a mask over his face, the blind metallic mask of Ares, sower of dragon's teeth. Where he let the seeds fall, forests would blacken, green vines wither, and smoke and destruction spring up.

There was no avoidance. Wholly fouled, one could not turn aside or swim away. Stone must be taken from stone and washed by the wind. Flesh and muscle must be separated from bone and washed clean. All must be freed of corruption, as the sea shells are burnished white by the sea and the sun.

Eleni no longer swam with the current. She was tired, and she let it carry her. Perhaps one day it would cast her up on Aphrodite's beach. She pictured herself there in the sea foam like a polished empty shell.

But it would not be like that. She would not be reborn or cleansed. She would be dead and horribly swollen, the way drowned things always are. A shiver went through her. To have vanity about one's dying was ridiculous, and still she felt it. Then the first mouthful of salt water burned her lungs, and she knew in a sudden stricken instant that she did not want to die.

Eleni struggled against the water, trying to lift herself. In the distance she saw a sail tacking behind the waves. She told herself it was Raphael coming back, but even if it were some other ship it was the last one she would ever see. The darkness would hide it soon.

She tried to swim for the beach, but fatigue and the gurgling wash of the current held her back. She was in the grip of the elements, and the elements were treacherous. A boat was her only chance, and that meant the lonely sail which dipped and disappeared and came again. She raised her arms to it, and sank lower, swallowing another fiery mouthful.

The sail grew, slowly. The storm would soon intervene, and with it the darkness. Already the sea wore brown scales from the rising wind. Again she raised her arm. "Please, God, please make him see me." She prayed as she had done during the fire. In the presence of death, she wanted to live.

The first few drops of rain pockmarked the water. There would be a lull as the line of boiling squall clouds passed over, and then the rain would descend in blinding torrent.

"Please, please . . . oh God! Please make him see me!" she said in her mind, for she dared not open her mouth.

The boat tacked nearer. It seemed purposeful in its approach, yet one long tack would carry it away. She waved. The figure at the helm made no sign, and gradually the boat turned into a ghost and vanished behind curtains of rain. Eleni gave one long choking shout and her voice was drowned. She saw neither ship nor helmsman again until the fishing boat was upon her. Heeling far over, it broke through the downpour and headed up, sails flapping. A fishing net came whirling down and she took hold of it. She had barely strength enough to hold on, but there were strong seaman's hands to haul her over the side.

Gasping, head down between her knees, Eleni sat in the caique. She had to brace herself as the wind filled the sails again and the boat headed off in the direction of New Paphos.

An old fisherman with hands like lobster claws grasped the helm. He did not speak or say anything about her swim. He was too busy steering and watching the water for gusts. She felt he understood everything and was grateful for his silence.

The rain fell in rattling sheets. The sails were heavy from it, and the fishing boat moved slowly as though through a lake of oil. The rain beat Eleni's hair down over her face, long dripping snakes of hair. The drops filled her eyes and at last she cried privately, for gratitude, for relief, for sorrow at last accepted and to be lived with. The tears came from the deepest parts of her, from every corner of her heart, and ran down her face with the rain.

They sailed toward New Paphos amid a ghost fleet of fishing boats, seen and not seen, amid the distant hails of fishermen and the conch horns blowing.

Leaning toward her, the old helmsman spoke for the first time. "You're the girl I've seen working on the beach with Raphael and that Turkish fellow, Jamal."

"Do you know them?"

"We passed them sailing out." For an unbelieving moment she imagined Jamal, risen, like Christ. "Said he was going to give the Turkish fellow a sea burial. Said he didn't want him folded up like a parcel and stuck into the ground."

That was right, she supposed, for the sea to claim her sailors. With soft green hands she would receive Jamal into her bosom.

Eleni asked whether Raphael had said anything about returning, but the boats had passed quickly on opposite tacks. Nothing more had been said. Still, Eleni knew that sooner or later he would return to Cyprus, as she had returned. Cyprus was home, no matter what.

•

The squall rolled over Cyprus. In the fire-gutted forests the rain sent up clouds of steam, and the fire fighters let it run like tears down their blackened faces. At the monastery, reverent hands lit all the candles before the iconostasis in thanksgiving. The forest would be saved. In the fields outside New Paphos, British soldiers poked through the desolated ruins of an ancient tomb. They found nothing alive, nothing to salvage. In a bed at New Paphos a woman breathed more easily with the cooling of the air. On the beach, fishermen drove their tarred caiques ashore and began to load straw baskets with their catch. The fish were lively and hard to handle because of the rain, and some of them flopped away and escaped into the sea.

Eleni left the old fisherman. She walked home through the crumbling gate of the fortress, down the street of the Turkish quarter. There it was quiet. She heard no voices behind the closed doors. The fighting was over. For a while people would have to rest, but she had no illusions. One could take their guns away and people would fight with their hands and feet. Cut off their hands and feet and, snakelike, they would attack one another. But for a time, while they rested, she would put out to sea in her own ship, that solitary vessel which is the artist's life. No longer, for good or bad, would she intrude on the lives of others, but as an artist she would try to explore the distant horizons and bring back fragments of what was true and beautiful. Like Raphael, she would be a seeker; perhaps never a finder, but a seeker in the sea of life until her eyes were sealed.

From the Turkish quarter she took the road which ran from the mountains to the sea. The rain had laid the dust and left puddles in the ruts. Ahead of her she saw her home, its whitewash cleansed by the storm, and beside it the darkly silhouetted chapel where Father Grikos had preached. Within, faint candles guttered before the iconostasis. A priest was lighting them.

"Father Constantine!"

The priest turned to her. With the candlelight searching his weary face he reminded Eleni of an old and misused camel. Still, he managed to smile.

"Eleni . . . All will be well, Eleni . . . I've seen your mother . . . and the forest is saved . . ." He had been lighting little flames to celebrate the end of the greater fire.

She asked him if he intended to stay in Paphos. He replied half-jokingly that he would stay to control the lighting of fires.

"What a filthy place this chapel has become!" he remarked. He would summon a battalion of village women to clean it. "And that great blank on the wall." Could she paint a picture to fill it?

Eleni promised to try. Already in her mind she had expunged the mad priest's painting. She would begin a new shield of Achilles, painting Cyprus as it ought to be, in sunshine, not in fire and blood.

Eastward lay the Troodos Mountains. Eleni could barely distinguish them. Except for the cedar forest drinking up the milky night, they might have been part of the sky. She would paint them at the center, brilliant under the sun. Westward she could see the black vineyards, and beyond them, countless stars. On the breeze was borne the taste of the sea. The sea would be part of her creation, blue, mysterious, all-encompassing. She had swam out to give up her life to the sea, and there, in the sea, she had been reborn. She would not again deny the world.